Chamán

The Universe is Ours

B.N. Armas

Written Words Publishing LLC
P.O. Box 462622
Aurora, Colorado 80046
www.writtenwordspublishing.com

Published by Written Words Publishing LLC January 18, 2025.

ISBN: 978-1-961610-26-2 (paperback)
ISBN: 978-1-961610-27-9 (hardcover)
ISBN: 978-1-961610-28-6 (eBook)
ISBN: 978-1-961610-29-3 (audiobook)

Library of Congress Control Number: 2024924939

This is a work of fiction. All events and characters in this story are solely the product of the author's imagination. Any similarities between any characters and situations presented in this story to any individuals living or dead or actual places and situations are pure coincidence.

Manufactured and printed in the United States of America

ACKNOWLEDGEMENTS

My mom, Carol, and my grandfather, Toribio Varela,
inspired this story.

It's dedicated to all my family—past and present.

As a Native American author, this fictional novel is to honor
all Indigenous Peoples who are the original stewards of the
lands on which we live.

"Just as a tree without roots is dead, a people without history or cultural roots also becomes a dead people."
– Malcom X

1

A STAR IS BORN

"The American Indian is of the soil, whether it be the region of forests, plains, pueblos, or mesas. He fits into the landscape, for the hand that fashioned the continent also fashioned the man for his surroundings. He once grew as naturally as the wild sunflowers. He belongs just as the buffalo belongs"
– Luther Standing Bear

"There is no fear in love, but perfect love drives out fear, because fear involves punishment. The one who fears is not made perfect in love."
– John 4:18 (BSB)

In the not so distant future, in a dark, majestic, gray castle located in Solorio, three people are sitting at a large wooden table in complete silence. The shimmering light from two five-arm candelabras on the table is the only movement in the room. A pleasant, woody aroma of incense wafts through the humid air.

Zapponata is a light-skinned, Middle Eastern woman in her eighties who is cursed with a black wart on her nose. With dark piercing eyes, she stares at her sixty-year-old son, Valdivinar.

Valdivinar is from Satan's seed. The entire Middle East has been under his rule for seven years. Some religious scholars label him the Antichrist. He stands over six feet tall, wearing a black suit and shirt with a matching black tie. His black mustache, short, curly hair, beady black eyes, and bushy eyebrows accent his ivory-complected evil face.

His thirty-year-old son, Drumpenfeurer, relaxes in his chair at the far end of the table drinking directly from a bottle of Osborn Whiskey. He has short straight hair and favors his father. The orange suit and tie match his reckless personality. He's the Commander of the very dangerous Mother Spaceship, La Mata Raza, an enormous gray vessel that transports one hundred single-pilot jet bombers. He's led hundreds of attacks worldwide with his bloodthirsty assassins.

After a long wait, the Prince of Darkness appears; a tall, thin man with gray eyes that match the color of his short, curly hair. Two small black horns protrude from the top of his forehead. He has a long, gray goatee. He's wearing a silk, floor-length dark maroon robe.

As he wanders among them, he says, "Welcome, my disgraceful family. You are all so incompetent. Have you found him yet?"

"Well, not exactly," Drumpenfeurer chimes in.

"Silence," the Prince of Darkness roars in anger as the table shakes.

Sweat begins to drip down Valdivinar's forehead.

"It's been foretold by the Great Creator that the Redeemer will come to defeat us. You've been looking for him in the wrong places. I've been searching the world for this child. I found him. I want you to attack this place tomorrow night. Everyone must die, grandson," the Prince of

Darkness commands as he hands Drumpenfeurer a crumpled piece of paper.

Drumpenfeurer looks at the coordinates. He rises and walks out the door. Zapponata and Valdivinar watch him leave without saying a word.

A beautiful Apache baby boy is born in Silver City, New Mexico. His bronze skin glows under the large, white chandelier as an Apache doula lifts him high in the air. His mother, Trinidad, admires him for the first time with a huge smile.

Trinadad is a beautiful young, NASA Space Engineer and Apache woman. She was raised on an Apache reservation until the age of five.

"Is he okay?" Trinidad asks the doula.

"Yes, Mom. He is looking very healthy," Maria responds.

She carefully cuts the umbilical cord. Clothed in a brown Indigenous dress with eagle feathers, she's not only there to assist in the birth, but also to provide a measure of comfort and safety, which reflects Apache culture. It is well known that Indigenous women have long been respected as life-givers.

"Oh, please give him to me," Trinidad says, exhausted after twelve hours of labor. Her long, jet-black hair is tangled and messy.

Maria carefully hands her the baby. As she holds him for the first time, the pleasant smell of soap, milk and fresh bread fills the room.

"Welcome, little one. My beautiful baby boy. You're so precious. I can't believe how lucky I am to have you. How are you?" Trinidad exclaims while gazing at her baby.

They're stationed in an underground fortress a hundred feet below the surface. Designed and built by NASA for the family's protection, it is the last of NASA's secret bomb shelters and is well protected by hundreds of well-trained Marines and Apache Warriors from the nearby Reservations. Suddenly, bombs begin igniting nearby.

"Oh, Great Creator, protect us," Trinidad gasps as the baby cries aloud.

Vibrations from the exploding missiles jolt the bedroom. Her baby stops crying and opens one eye, showing no emotion. It's almost as if he understands evil is revealing its true colors.

Trinidad looks at the bedroom monitor. She sees green and red flashes of missiles in the air.

"My baby. They're not taking you from me. I'll protect you."

Her beloved husband, Commander Maximus Hogan, is watching everything from his monitor aboard La Azteca, the largest spaceship NASA has ever built. He's standing inside the Command Center. Through a large window, he can also see Planet Samra, one hundred and fifty million miles from Earth. Each month, hundreds of thousands flee to this wonderful planet that millions of evacuees now call home.

Maximus is six feet six inches tall. His bronze-colored face and long, dark ponytail bring out his Native American features. He's thankful for the good health of Trinidad and his new baby boy. He wishes he could be there, but it's a ten-day excursion to and from Samra.

He appears on the monitor and says, "I'm so proud of you, my love. You did it, Trinidad. He's so beautiful."

"We did it, my love," she says, feeling a little tired.

Her mother-in-law, Dr. Melissa Hogan, a sixty-nine-year-old NASA Apache scientist, is sitting in a rocking chair, witnessing the moment. She gets up to look at her new grandson. Her long white hair and purple dress make her appear majestic. Her ageless face is dark brown. Her fervent belief in medicinal herbs is well-known to all. A cup of Echinacea tea sits on the table beside her.

Her husband, seventy-year-old Dr. Matthew Hogan, stands as he walks toward his grandson. NASA hired him as their Chief Space Scientist and Senior Climate Advisor. He's an extremely fit, dark brown Apache. Both live inside the same compound. He has written several books on climate change on Earth and other planets for which he won a Pulitzer Prize.

The flickering fireplace is kept going through the night, only twenty feet away. Even though it is the coldest day of the year, the room temperature is a comfortable twenty-one degrees Celsius.

"He's so beautiful. He looks like you," Melissa says with a big smile.

"Congratulations, my dear," Matthew says with a huge grin.

Just then, the room begins rocking back and forth from the bombing. The magnificent crystal chandelier falls near Trinadad's bed and the large collection of books spills out of the bookcase.

Maria screams, "Dios mio," and quickly begins picking up pieces of glass and books from the floor.

Cochise, Trinidad's robot guard, opens the bedroom door and enters. He's an Indigenous android designed to resemble the famous Apache Chief. At six feet seven inches, he towers over everyone. He's dressed in modest brown tasseled pants with moccasins and no shirt. His long black ponytail hangs down to the middle of his back. A red and black headband crowns his head.

Maximus asks, "Is everyone okay?"

Trinidad speaks in Athabascan, "We're okay. Cochise, go see Carol. Follow her orders. She will tell you what to do to save us. Hurry."

"Yes, ma'am," he answers without hesitation.

Cochise runs to the secret NASA Command Center where Carol is located. The station is well hidden from satellite detection, due to the ten-foot-thick lead walls. Carol is the supercomputer in charge of giving commands for airstrikes. Its knowledge is derived from NASA's satellites. Everyone listens to her for instructions.

Twenty NASA engineers are monitoring the missile attack on two large screens at their stations. Cochise launches the Patriot Defensive Missile Attack Plan as Carol instructed him. He presses a big, red, mushroom-shaped button inside a silver panel mounted on the front wall. Fifteen minutes later, the enemy spaceships are caught by surprise. They quickly retreat and are out of range in minutes.

Carol the supercomputer announces on an intercom to everyone in the bedroom, "The enemy threat is gone. You are safe. Cochise did a magnificent job launching our missiles from the White Apache Mountain just as planned. They weren't ready for it."

"Thank you, Carol. Without your help, everyone would have died," Maximus replies.

Trinidad is glowing with joy, especially since they survived another missile attack by Drumpenfeurer's fleet.

Native Americans believe that giving birth is sacred. Trinidad continues to nurse the baby with mixed emotions—the moment for her is precious, but she also feels sad and confused because she knows her child is the target. Holding back her emotions, she tries valiantly to display courage to everyone in the room, especially her baby.

"I wish I had been there, my love," Maximus tells her. "Fortunately, Carol warned us and it looks like the enemy has left the quadrant. They weren't able to find the exact location of our space station, thank God."

"I know. What do we do with our baby? They'll eventually find us."

"All of you need to come to Samra," Maximus pleads.

"We can't. The President has ordered us to stay."

"I know. I've asked him to let you come to your new home. It's a lovely place for all of us. However, he needs you there to help with the evacuation for the time being. The evil Zapponata broke our treaty. She doesn't want anyone to leave Earth. She wants them as slaves."

Carol says, "I heard she wants everyone back from Samra."

"Never. We're here to stay. Let's change the subject," Maximus suggested. "We should take this moment to enjoy our new baby boy. He looks amazing. He's such a beautiful baby. What do you think of the name Magnus?" he asks Trinidad.

"I love that name. Hi, Magnus. Do you like your name?" Trinidad teases him.

Everyone watches the dark-haired baby breastfeed with his eyes closed.

Meanwhile, their six-year-old daughter is preparing to join her family. Dahteste is named after a very famous Apache woman. She is fair-skinned with long black hair and green eyes. Wearing a silver space outfit, she walks out of her bedroom and begins heading down the seemingly interminable stretch of corridor to see her new baby brother. Excitedly, she stumbles, falling to the floor before opening the large wooden double doors. There she sees her mom lying in bed, nursing her brother.

"Hello, Dahteste. How are you doing?" Maximus asks.

"Hi, Daddy. I'm scared. When are you coming home?"

"I'll be home soon, sweety," he calmly replies.

Trinidad's seven-year-old son, Itza-Chu, meaning Great Eagle, walks into the room. His long black hair partially covers his bronze skin.

"Mom, can I see my brother?" he asks, yawning.

"Of course, Itza-Chu. But don't make any noise. Say 'hi' to your father."

"Oh, hi Dad," Itza-Chu says, flippantly.

"Son, what's wrong?" Maximus asks.

"Where are you?" his son snapped.

"Itza-Chu, don't talk to your dad that way. You say you're sorry right now," Trinidad demands.

Itza-Chu pauses and then looks up at the monitor on the wall. "I'm sorry," he says. "Father, why are they trying to kill us?"

"Itza-Chu, I accept your apology. I'm very proud of you and Dahteste. Don't ever forget that. Right now, I am in my spaceship guarding the newly built city of El Castillo on Planet Samra. This is the most beautiful planet you'll ever see. The sky is orange and the land teems with colorful trees, flowers, sand, and water. I have a hacienda that you will live in one day," Maximus says, smiling proudly.

Trinidad's gaze is fixed on her husband. Her eyes are sparkled with love and admiration as she blows him a kiss.

"Son, you must stay strong," Maximus continues. "This will end eventually. Let's enjoy this day. You have a new brother and his name is Magnus," he says with great pride.

"Magnus?" Dahteste shouts with joy as she touches his little arm.

Itza-Chu walks up to him and touches his black hair, proud to see his baby brother and only hoping that Magnus would not be the center of his mother's attention for long. For the rest of the day, however, they shared their affection for the baby boy.

Zapponata is back in the Prince of Darkness' castle, still in an orange gown. He is smoking a cigar and sitting in a large black chair. She kneels before him, kissing his hand.

"Master, we didn't kill Maximus' baby. I'm sorry."

"Worthless woman. Don't tell me what I already know. What I need to hear from you is that he's dead. Do you understand?" he adds with a growl.

The Prince of Darkness points at her and she vanishes from the room. He lurks about, still smoking his cigar. Suddenly, he pulls it from his mouth and throws it on the dark wooden floor.

2

LA FAMILIA

"Everything on Earth is Borrowed…There is no 'Mine' or
'Yours'…there is Only 'Ours'…Even Time is Borrowed. We Kill
over a Plot of Land that belongs only to our Mother Earth.
All you have is what you came with…and what you
will leave with…Your Spirit."
– Native American Proverb

Five years later, Maximus' family is in an underground shelter in Silver City, New Mexico. Magnus is playing with a toy truck next to Dahteste and Itza-Chu. They all wear a Mickey Mouse T-shirt. Trinidad is reading a book to them about Geronimo, a great Apache Leader. Maximus lies in bed listening. His mom and dad walk in.

"Good morning, everyone," Melissa says.

"Good morning, Grandma and Grandpa," all three kids shout.

Dahteste suddenly stands, picking up a picture from a bureau. "Mommy, please tell us about this picture."

Trinidad looks at it and smiles. "I'm so proud of your father in his favorite gold uniform. I like the red, white and blue United States flag embroidered sharply on it. The black laser blaster was given to him by the owner of NASA. The golden crown with a turquoise stone was a gift from his Apache people."

Dahteste says, "I like his long black hair, beard and mustache."

"Yes, he always likes to keep it nice and neat for me. Look how strong his arms and legs are. He loves to work out," Trinidad says, smiling.

Dahteste picks up another picture and asks, "How about this one, Mommy?"

"Well, your father played baseball for the Los Angeles Dodgers. His brothers played baseball, too. You can see them all together in their uniforms. He pitched and played for ten years before getting hurt. His arm injury caused him to retire at an early age."

"How about this one?" Itza-Chu asks while holding the picture he found on a larger brown wooden bureau.

"Baseball was the love of his life when he was young. Here he is at seven years old. This is your Grandpa Matthew Hogan who coached him in Little League, Pony League and Colt League," Trinidad lovingly explains.

"Who is this boxer?" Itza-Chu asks.

"His nickname was Meedee. He was a professional boxer. Your dad trained with him. They ran up and down the rugged mountains around the border town of San Ysidro. He grew up there."

Maximus interrupts, "I would often run with sandals through sandy roads lined with jumping cacti and dry brush. There were days when I ran the course alone in the dark. Undocumented immigrants would be either hiding in the bushes or running from 'La Migra.' They chased them in their green and white SUVs. There were some horrific moments that I witnessed as a young man."

"What is La Migra, Daddy?" Dahteste asks.

"Well, first poor people came to this country looking for a better way of life. They immigrated to escape poverty and injustice in their countries. However, some were harshly greeted by young men with guns. I saw Border Patrol helicopters swarming mercilessly over immigrant families detained on the railroad tracks at night, as well. The pilots would yell repeatedly at the top of their lungs, 'Don't move! Stay on the ground, wetbacks!' Their intercom was so loud it kept me from sleeping. I looked out my bedroom window and saw scared families surrounded by border agents—La Migra.

"All people are human and should be treated respectfully and given equal opportunity. Indigenous people born in the Americas being called 'aliens' in America makes no sense to me. We were the first ones on this continent. No one 'discovered' this country. It was given to us by the Great Creator. Our Lady of Guadalupe Treaty in 1848 between the United States and Mexico established the rights of Indigenous Americans to live on Turtle Island."

Melissa stands up. She walks toward a big picture on the wall. "Look at this picture," she says. "Your father is with President Johnny Long Feather. He was the fifth Indigenous President of the United States. The country was never stronger. He was our greatest President. He united everyone with his words of wisdom. There was world peace while he was in office. He taught that fear is the cause of hate. Love is the only way to conquer it."

She points with her right index finger to a picture of Maximus wearing an eagle feather headband and standing outside a teepee. "I took this picture when he was twelve at an Apache Village near Silver City, New Mexico. We enjoyed going there. We formed strong bonds with our relatives and gained a better understanding of who we are as the First Nations People. He learned a great deal about Apache culture, its art forms and its stories. Always remember that blood is thicker than water. In the village, most people are related to each other. We must protect each other. We need to keep a lookout so we can all stay out of danger."

"Wow," Dahteste astonishingly replies. "We are good people."

"Yes, we are," Melissa says. "Here's your great-great-grandfather. You can tell by looking at his long black hair and high cheekbones, he had Indigenous blood in him. He was a great man. As a full-blooded Apache, he was six foot four inches tall. You can see your father looks like him."

"All of us called him Tata," Trinidad adds. "I want you to know that you have Apache and Navajo blood. You should be proud of your roots."

"Yes, children," Maximus proudly says. "Even though I'm not 100% Indigenous—my *heart* is."

"This is one of my favorites," Melissa says. "It's your father's college graduation picture. He earned a Space Engineering Degree from San Diego State University. He gave a commencement speech to the graduating class. I'll never forget that day. He's not only smart, but brave. Once your father decides to do something, nothing can stop him. He's not a quitter."

Trinidad interjects, "Something else he likes is watching classic movies."

Maximus interrupts, "To this day, I love watching *Dances With Wolves, Field of Dreams, Once Upon A Time in Hollywood,*

Scarface, The Godfather, Close Encounters of the Third Kind, Star Wars, Indiana Jones and the Last Crusade, The Mask, and all Batman and Superman movies."

The children laugh because they love watching their favorite cartoons like Mickey Mouse and Minnie Mouse. The young siblings are sitting Indian-style on the white rug enjoying this moment of show-and-tell.

Their grandmother says, "Your dad has worked at NASA as the Space Commander of the Planet Samra Space Station Program for fifteen years. He is the leader in developing and implementing the plan to evacuate people from Earth. He also oversees building cities on the planet. That's what he does when he's not home. Everything he does saves lives. One day, we'll be going with him to Samra."

"Really, Grandma. When can we go?" Dahteste asks.

Trinidad says, "You'll be going with your father soon. I promise."

"Yay," all three children smile and high-five each other.

"Would you like to learn how the planet was discovered?" Melissa asks.

Itza-Chu says, "Yes, please tell us, Grandma."

"Our NASA engineers discovered several planets that might have life, however, they didn't know what type of life. Our astronauts found an exoplanet almost entirely covered by water. They thought we might be able to live there. The atmosphere has the right amount of oxygen, nitrogen, carbon dioxide, and water vapor, with trace amounts of other gases— just like here on Earth. The hydrosphere is warmed by solar energy like ours. It has the same temperature. Other elements like phosphorus and sulfur are found in abundance."

"Grandma, we don't understand what you're saying," Itza- Chu says in confusion.

"One day, you will. Do you want me to stop?"

"No, please keep going. I like the story about Samra," Itza-Chu says.

"Okay. The ground has the basic components of soil with organic matter and seventy percent water. When they first discovered Samra, they didn't know if anyone lived on the planet."

"How far is it, Grandma?" Dahteste asks.

"That is a good question," she says with a smile.

Dahteste slugs Itza-Chu in the stomach. Both start giggling and wrestling on the carpet next to Magnus.

Trinidad says, "Children, stop that. You don't want to hurt Magnus."

Itza-Chu stops wrestling as he looks at his mom. As Trinidad bends down to pick up Magnus from the rug, he feels sad that his mom is more concerned about Magnus than him.

"Well, after a lot of research and some luck, Samra is only ten days from here," Melissa says.

"Wow, that's a long time," Dahteste exclaims.

A huge laugh is heard in the room from Maximus and Matthew. Dahteste and Itza-Chu look dumbfounded by their laughter.

Maximus tries to please her by saying, "Dahteste, ten days is a very long time. We should find a way to get there quicker."

After a short pause, Trinidad says, "Children, ask your grandmother about this picture of your father dressed in a white astronaut custom-made space suit."

"Oh, yes," Melissa says. "This is the first secret mission to Samra. The picture was given to us by NASA. It was taken when he stepped off his spaceship, La Azteca, onto the planet for the first time. He was the first human ever to do this. How many times have you been there, mijo?" she asks him.

"Twenty-five times, children," Maximus explains. "One day, you'll see all our big buildings, beautiful trees, plants, oceans, rivers, and mountains. You'll love it. People live in peace and happiness. They play games and watch movies like us. They get to go outside and fly in their car planes. They can travel all over the planet to see the beautiful orange sky. It is truly a miracle."

"Wow," Itza-Chu says in awe.

"It took a supercomputer named Carol to make this happen. It is your mom's invention," Melissa adds in excitement.

The children turn around and look at their mom holding Magnus. She is looking at them nodding her head.

"Why did you call your computer 'Carol,' Mommy?" Dahteste asks.

"I named it Carol after my mom. She helped invent it," she says with a smile.

Trinidad pauses to think of her mother's tragic death. Unfortunately, she was killed in a missile attack a few days after Itza-Chu was born. She was in her hacienda-style home in Silver City, New Mexico when Drumpenfeurer bombed the city. Carol's husband, Golthli, an Apache Shaman, survived the bombing because he was in a Powwow in Yuma, Arizona.

She continues, "We invented a supercomputer to think like us. I think of it as a mom because it is super smart. When I talk about Carol, I remember my mom. Carol knows the history of every human on Earth. Also, it knows about the structure of the Earth and how to design buildings. It knows more about the universe and Samra than anyone. It is connected to our powerful satellites that constantly send live images and videos. Carol knows things before any of us. Without the super-computer, we wouldn't be able to survive."

Melissa is looking at the children who are enjoying the story. She is amazed that they are still awake.

"You see, the smartest people could only tell us there is a possibility of living on Samra. Carol is the mastermind that figured out the mathematical formula to live there and how to get there in ten days. Carol explained to us that there is plenty of oxygen and water vapor for a comfortable life on Samra. It can analyze other significant factors of life on any planet. Carol uses infrared and space telescope pictures that have been around for fifty years. It knows about light shot by a star through the atmosphere of a distant planet technique known as spectroscopy. It uses the slices missing from the light spectrum to tell us which chemicals or gases are present in the atmosphere around planets. After processing the bar codes of any atmosphere, Carol can tell us if life exists there."

Trinidad looks down at the children, asleep on the carpet.

Ten days later, Trinidad is in bed with Maximus. He's asleep as she reflects on when she attended the University of California Los Angeles (UCLA). She studied Space Engineering and Physics. Her classes taught her to understand the universe a little more. This involved design, development and operation of technologies and systems related to space exploration. Satellite communications and space-based research are the most important parts of the class that helped her invent Carol.

Her belief since childhood is that we are not alone in the universe. She was a curious child who liked asking questions.

She was raised with traditional Apache values on an Apache Reservation in New Mexico. Her mother was strong and wise. She taught her about medicinal herbs and her ancestry. As a child, Trinidad was always sick. She almost died of pneumonia after a very cold winter at the age of thirteen. She was cured with herbal teas after two ceremonial healing sweat lodge sessions.

The sweat lodge is a place of healing, renewal, resurrection, and communion. It is a sacred ritual that has little in common with other religious rituals. It is a great privilege to participate in the sacred ritual of a sweat lodge of the Apache people. Each healing ceremony takes four hours inside a small oval buffalo-skinned hut. She recalls the beautiful sage plant aroma. Tobacco was used outside the hut as a spiritual offering for the healing.

Inside the hut, one by one, hot boulders are placed into a shallow hole. Everyone sits Indian-style around them. The hut is held up with sturdy willow tree branches. The temperature inside the dark sweat lodge can reach one hundred fifty degrees. It's a ceremony that can cause high anxiety, especially if one is claustrophobic. In order to last four hours inside a dark, hot, enclosed hut, Indigenous elders believe that love must overcome fear in one's heart. It takes a lot of courage to participate in such a ritual, she thinks.

In Athabascan, her father prayed to the Great Creator for spiritual healing. He brushed her body with wet white sage. Afterward, he gave her medicinal herbs to lessen the mucus and fever. After a few days of sweat lodge ceremonies, the illness left her. She never forgot how she survived and who healed her. She is a quick learner and has a photographic memory. In high school, she excelled in math and science.

She would wake up at sunrise and run five miles every day.

She was taught this is good for her body and soul. She was the State champion in cross-country running. For this, she earned an academic scholarship to UCLA.

Trinidad met Maximus in an astronomy class he taught at the university. It was love at first sight for her. She was twenty-one and he was thirty. During his lectures, she would pretend to be listening to the planets' and stars' names but she couldn't help but think of him.

She remembers the blue jeans and white T-shirt he wore every day to class. He was clean-shaven with a long, black ponytail. Her favorite moment in class was when he would turn off the lights. He'd have everyone lean back in their chairs and stare at the dark ceiling. Then he'd illuminate the ceiling with the stars and planets of our solar system, pointing out the different constellations and star signs. With his looks and powerful voice, he had a commanding presence.

This was during her second year at UCLA. She normally wore dresses and red lipstick to class. She still had two more years. She enjoyed looking at her handsome young professor. With her head resting on her hand, she would sit at her desk and smile at him. Her bright brown eyes and skin glowed in the classroom light.

She remembered Maximus saying, "Welcome to Astronomy 101. If you haven't got the syllabus yet, it is on the classes' server. I have extra copies, but I have to say, I don't know where they are."

He looked around for some of his notes, clumsily knocking all the papers off the podium. Everyone laughed as the papers flew everywhere.

"Okay, astrologers observe that while the sky rotates during the night and slowly shifts over the year," Maximus said as he gained his composure. "Individual stars appear to be fixed in place within their constellations. However, planets are a different story. The word 'planet' comes from the Greek term 'to wander.' We know them as the Sun, the Moon, Mercury, Venus, Mars, Jupiter, and Earth."

After the lecture, she remembers him looking at her from the podium as she walked out of the classroom. At that moment she knew he was someone special.

3

CAROL

"Teach us love, compassion, and honor that we may
heal the earth and each other."
– Ojibwa Prayer

Five years after taking Astronomy 101, Trinidad is working for NASA, in Houston, Texas, as a Lead Engineer. She's walking down a corridor to meet her boss in her blue designer NASA nylon space outfit. Three logos adorn her shirt: a red space shuttle inside a black circle, a rectangular gray box with red wings and a round white circle with a bald eagle. Her black hair is long and straight down to her hips.

Maximus is now the Space Commander in charge of The Planet Samra Mission. He's walking to a meeting at NASA to discuss the mission. Arthur Little Feather, his young assistant, is walking beside him. Both are wearing a dark blue NASA uniform with a gold space shuttle logo. Maximus is sporting a full beard with his signature long, shiny, black ponytail. It's grown longer since his days as a college professor. Arthur is short with long black hair too. He's from an Apache tribe in New Mexico.

Trinidad turns the corner, texting her mother, as Maximus accidentally bumps her hand with his left arm and her cell phone drops to the gold marble floor.

"I'm sorry, miss," he says as he bends down to pick it up. As he looks up, he sees her staring at him in shock.

She stammers, "Professor Maximus?"

"Trinidad?" he asks, surprised.

"Yes, remember me from your astronomy class?" she inquires politely.

"Of course. How could I forget a smart student like you? What are you doing here?"

"I'm working on the Exoplanet Exploration Project," she responds nervously.

"Really? I am too. I hope I didn't break your phone."

Maximus stares at her. He can't believe how beautiful she looks. She's more mature and attractive since he last saw her.

"No, it's working," she replies as she presses a couple of buttons.

They look at each other and smile.

"This is my first day. What do you do here?" Trinidad asks while stroking her hair.

"I'm working on the Samra Space Project."

"Wow, what is that about?" she asks.

Arthur interrupts, looking at his watch, "We have a meeting with General Stewart in five minutes, Maximus."

"Arthur, tell General Stewart I am sorry, but I need to take care of an urgent matter."

"What matter are you talking about, sir?" he asks politely.

Maximus and Trinidad just gaze at each other and Arthur gets the hint.

"I'll let him know," he adds, walking away.

Maximus and Trinidad are in a hypnotic state. It feels as

if fate has brought them together.

Maximus asks, "Do you have some time right now?"

"Time for what?"

"My apologies. I'm looking for help with this new project. Would you like to see what I'm doing?"

She pauses before adding, "May I call my supervisor to let him know?"

"Who's your supervisor?"

"Dr. Junior Robles."

"That's funny," Maximus laughs. "I'm *his* supervisor. Let him know you'll be with me for the rest of the day, if that's okay?"

"Of course," she replies with a huge smile.

Maximus and Trinidad are now inside NASA's Command Space Station viewing four large screens. Twenty engineers are working at their stations, receiving space satellite data on their computers.

"Have you been here before, Trinidad?" Maximus asks.

"No, I haven't. What is this project about?"

He replies with a grin from ear to ear, "Do you see that planet on the screen?"

Trinidad looks with fascination at a dark purple planet on the monitor.

"Well, that planet, according to our research, may be the future of mankind. We are ninety-five percent sure it has all the elements for life according to infrared and telescopic data," he excitedly tells her.

"Really? I can't believe it. Is there anything I can do to help you? It's been a dream I've had all my life to prove that there's life on other planets."

"Maybe," Maximus replies. "Tell me more about yourself. Weren't you Class Valedictorian?"

Trinidad thinks back on her graduation day at UCLA. She is dressed in a beautiful blue and white graduation gown, a blue cap and tassel placed perfectly on her head. Her long black hair is symbolic of her native heritage. According to Apaches, the longer the hair, the greater the strength. Also, it is a symbol of a strong cultural identity to the tribe. It helps her self-esteem and self-respect and provides a sense of belonging.

She was taught by her mom about the cleanliness of the body. Well-groomed hair—with or without ornaments—is greatly valued by the Indigenous family. Long hair reinforces her connection with her native brothers and sisters. On this day, she has adorned her hair with an eagle feather.

The President of UCLA says, "Now, let me introduce Trinidad Barela, your Class Valedictorian."

Everyone stands and applauds.

"Earth to Trinidad. Are you there, over?" Maximus jokes.

"When you asked me that question, I remembered that special day. I'm sorry. It makes me very emotional," she explains.

"During your commencement speech, you spoke about space exploration and your dream that people would one day live on another planet. I remember the standing ovation from your fellow graduates. The faculty and everyone in the audience stood and cheered. How did that make you feel?"

"You remember my speech?" she asks, surprised. "It made me feel like the luckiest person on the planet."

"Your speech motivated me to have the same dream. How could I ever forget it?"

She tells him all about her life since she was a little girl. Her life story touches Maximus.

"I'm so lucky to have met you at this point in my life," he says, gazing into her bright, brown, glazed eyes.

He feels she could help him with The Planet Samra Mission and she happily agrees to join his team. Both politely hug and walk out of the Space Center.

Two years later, Maximus and Trinidad are still together at NASA. They've been working on sending the first man to Samra during this time. At Philipi's Pizza Restaurant, they're about to have a pepperoni pizza with a dinner salad. Before they begin, Maximus gets on one knee and shows her a small black jewelry box hidden in his Levi jacket. He opens it as people stare.

Maximus asks nervously, "Will you marry me, Trinidad Barela?"

She looks at him with tears in her eyes and says, "That depends."

"On what?" he asks, confused.

"Will you take me with you to a distant land that our Great Spirit put in my heart since I was a child?"

"Trinidad, I will take you there one day. I promise we will be there together for eternity. You have my word," he lovingly responds.

"Well, then of course I'll marry you," Trinidad shrieks as people applaud.

Two years have passed since their small Native American wedding in San Ysidro, California. There were Indigenous dancers at the reception at Balboa Park —an unforgettable experience.

They're with their baby, Itza-Chu, in their coastal bedroom in Imperial Beach, California. As they're getting ready for another day of work, they see on their wall-mounted television a news breaking report flashing on the screen.

"Breaking News from Russia today," a male newscaster reports. "Russian cosmonauts have discovered a new black hole in the universe near T1001. Russian scientists believe this could be a porthole to other galaxies."

Maximus says excitedly, "Could this be the corridor that can expedite voyages to Samra? We need to find out. When we get to NASA, work with my mom and your new supercomputer Carol. Carol needs to get the coordinates. Once it has them, then it can tell us everything about the black hole."

"Maybe this is the final piece of the puzzle. This could get us to Samra a lot faster," Trinidad says.

"Right now, it would take five light years to reach it. I hope you're right. Only Carol can give us that answer," Maximus says.

Trinidad and Melissa are in their NASA laboratory giving Carol the black hole coordinates near T1001. They also input the spherical topology and dynamical stability of the area.

Trinidad says, "Most scientists believe that black holes may be the portal that connects other planets of the universe, or other universes entirely. However, this is pure speculation."

Melissa says, "I've read about the same thing from

prominent scientists. Trinidad, don't forget to ask Carol how the black hole could impact linear time...or if time there is fluid...if it fluctuates."

"Those are excellent questions, Mother Hogan."

Once the data is provided to Carol, they see Earth and Samra with the black hole in between the large wall-mounted screen.

Carol says, "Black Hole T1001 is a cosmic body, which has existed for millions of years. According to universal data, this is a portal to reach the Samra in ten days. Time is unaffected. In other words, the black hole won't alter time. Earth's gravitational pull is approximately ten meters per second. Samra's gravitational pull is the same. Congratulations on finding a faster means of traveling to Samra."

"This is a historic moment for mankind," Melissa says. "Carol is the only machine this advanced. We owe you so much, Carol. You are amazing."

Tears are streaming down Trinidad's face as she says, "My dream has come true because of Carol. I can't believe it. Now, we must start evacuating people to Samra before it's too late."

Melissa adds, "Samra is our only hope of continued existence in the universe. Our planet has collapsed and has become a wasteland. Zapponata and her family's war against the world cannot be stopped. This great adventure took more than a man could ever comprehend. Thank you, Carol. No human could do what you've done."

"We will be known for the tracks we leave. We are on our way," Trinidad shouts as she hugs her mother-in-law.

4

The Beginning of the End

*"It is better to have less thunder in the mouth
and more lightning in the hand."*
– Apache Tribe Proverb

Maximus and Trinidad are at home in Imperial Beach, California, anxiously waiting for orders to evacuate people to Samra. La Azteca will be used for the mission as it is capable of housing five thousand people.

Dahteste is one-year-old. Her and Itza-Chu are awake in a playpen in the living room. Their parents are in the kitchen drinking coffee and eating cream-filled donuts. The kitchen is painted white with crown molding, with ceramic roosters hanging from a brass cage in the center of it. Their stainless-steel appliances are all solar-operated by means of a small solar chip. All electrical power is generated this way.

Both are standing looking out of their open sliding glass door, enjoying the gentle ocean breeze. They can smell the saltwater and hear the Pacific Ocean waves crashing on the huge gray rocks five hundred feet from their home. Seven black and white Pelicans are flying in a V formation above them. Children are playing tag on the sand. People are fishing on the long old wooden pier. It's another beautiful sunny day in America's finest city. Unfortunately, Maximus and Trinidad know the evil Zapponata has been relentlessly bombing locations worldwide for the past three years. No one is safe.

Trinidad says, "We need to start evacuating people to Samra, Maximus. This world is too dangerous to bring up a family. I believe life would be better for our children there. What do we need to do to get this going?"

"I agree," Maximus says while looking at the ocean waves. "We've waited too long for the President to give us the green light. Everything is ready to start building a new city on the planet. The plan is in place. All we need to do is implement it."

"I'll get the kids ready. Maybe today is the day. We must leave in twenty minutes or we'll be late for our meeting in Houston."

Trinidad walks into the living room as Maximus goes to their bedroom to change into his NASA outfit. Even though NASA is in Texas, they have a solar-powered, six-passenger space car that takes them to work in under an hour. The rainbow-colored vehicle is connected to Carol who can inform them of any danger.

They're outside their beautiful white house. Trinidad is buckling Dahteste into the car seat as Maximus does the same with Itza-Chu. Maximus and Trinidad start singing *This Land Is Your Land* as they lift off the platform in their front yard. Two minutes later, a loud explosion is heard and a giant mushroom-shaped white cloud rises towards their space car.

"Quick, let's hurry up," Trinidad says.

The deafening noise causes temporary hearing loss so Maximus doesn't hear a word she says. However, he understands the need to leave the area if they wish to survive. He presses a red button labeled "Jet Power" and, within seconds, they are far from the blast.

Maximus is finally heard asking, "Are you okay, Trinidad?"

"Yes, I am. Are you?" she replies in a daze.

"I'm okay."

Dahteste screams and starts to cry.

"Don't worry, honey," Trinidad comforts her.

"How's Itza- Chu?" Maximus asks.

"He's hurt."

Trinidad turns to comfort them. Itza-Chu is bleeding from his forehead. She grabs a handkerchief from her brown bag and wipes the blood trickling down his face. He has a large lump after hitting his head on the space car window. She thinks he's badly hurt. He doesn't make a sound.

"Commander Maximus, come in, over," Carol says from the monitor.

"This is Maximus, over."

"Thank God you're okay. How are Trinidad and the children?" Carol asks.

"Itza-Chu has a swollen head and his forehead is bleeding. We're going to take him to emergency once we arrive in Houston," Maximus replies.

"Okay. I hope it's not serious. I just saw the missile erupt in your neighborhood. It took out everything. I'm sad to tell you but your home was the target. The magnitude eleven missiles and their compounds are of Russian design. The enemy Mother Ship La Mata Raza was seen in the area minutes before the explosion," Carol explains.

"Carol, please have everyone meet me in the Command Space Center room in one hour," Maximus says in earnest.

Carol replies, "San Diego is seen as a ghost town with smoldering buildings and rubble. There is virtually no one left. The missiles traveled one thousand miles per hour and could not be detected by our satellites in time. We couldn't stop them. The Coronado Bridge is collapsing into the Pacific Ocean. More than five million people have perished. A Tsunami over one thousand feet high swallowed up America's finest city. You can see the devastation on your monitor in five seconds."

As Maximus and Trinidad watch the devastation on the monitor, they arrive at a hospital in Houston. They quickly take both children into the emergency room.

The high-powered satellites project live videos down to NASA's Command Space Center. NASA engineers, scientists, Maximus, and Trinidad silently watch in shock. San Diego has become the latest desolate city in the world. Their mouths drop.

The President of the United States is seen being evacuated from the bunker at the White House. Her family, employees and Generals run across the grass to the Presidential helicopter. They arrive at the airport where they board Air Force One. All are now safely in the air.

President Angela Little Cloud enters her office with General Musgrove by her side. She is a beautiful, middle-aged Navajo woman in a beige dress. Her long, black straight hair is hanging down her back. Her striking voice exudes confidence. When she speaks, everyone listens.

"Get me that dictator on the line," she demands.

"He's on the line, Madam President," her secretary announces from the intercom.

"Valdivinar?" she says on the speakerphone with General Musgrove and her military staff present.

"Yes, Madam President," he answers courteously.

"We just had a massive bombing that destroyed San Diego, California. What do you know about this?"

Valdivinar is in his mansion in the Middle East, sitting in his office in a black suit, shirt and matching black tie. His coarse, heavily accented voice is hard to understand. He has everyone's attention as he appears on the President's monitor.

"Madam President, I want to assure you that I had nothing to do with it," he says.

"You know what happened, Valdivinar. Why did you do this? We've lost over five million lives and the finest city in our country," she sternly tells him.

"Come now, Madam President. Do you think I could do such a thing?"

"I don't think. I *know* you did it," she shouts in anger.

Just then, General Musgrove approaches her and whispers into her ear, "Madam President, La Mata Raza is within striking distance of our plane. Our intelligence told us Drumpenfeurer is onboard and he's ready to attack. Do you know that he's Valdivinar's son? What do we do?"

The President's eyes are wide open and she looks around at her staff. She pauses and then regains her composure.

"Dictator Valdivinar, why is La Mata Raza in our air space? Tell your son to leave or we will shoot him down in ten seconds," she commands.

Valdivinar smiles and says, "Goodbye, Madam President," as he presses a red button on his computer.

A giant explosion is heard in the sky and a cloud of the white powder is seen. Air Force One is gone.

"Is everyone here?" Maximus asks his staff and engineers as he stands inside the Command Space Center.

Sitting around their stations, the space engineers are angry and scared. Trinidad and Melissa are visibly shaken, anxiously awaiting details from Carol. As everyone looks at the large monitors on the wall, Valdivinar appears on the screen, angry and frustrated.

"Maximus, my mother has given you every chance in the world to surrender," he says.

"Valdivinar, so you're behind all of this?" Maximus says in a strong commanding voice.

"You are very elusive. I see you're still alive. Congratulations. I hope you won't take it personally. We could still be friends if you join our forces."

"With friends like you, who needs enemies, son of all evil? You know you just signed your death warrant, right?" Maximus fiercely says.

"Maximus, how are you going to attack me without a leader? Where is your President?" he laughs.

Carol announces, "The President was onboard Air Force One five minutes ago and it's been reported missing."

Valdivinar laughs malevolently on the monitor. "Don't look at me," he says jokingly.

Carol says, "Drumpenfeurer's spacecraft, La Mata Raza, lasered it down five minutes ago, according to our satellite video."

Everyone watches the replay of the President's aircraft

exploding. Some of the engineers in the room begin to scream in fear. This is a frightening moment in the history of the United States. The country is facing imminent destruction.

Valdivinar says, "Let this be a lesson to you, Yankees. Your President didn't listen and she paid the price. You better hope your Vice President will bow down to me. All he needs to do is kneel before me and swear his allegiance. He will declare that I am now your Commander and Chief. Finally, he'll need to give me the power to control the military, the missiles, navy ships, aircraft, satellites, and his army."

Vice President Sparky Carlson is a tall, dark-skinned, white-haired, fifty-year-old man dressed in a blue suit, white shirt and blue tie. He was born in Arizona to an African American father and Apache mother. He has just been sworn in as President a few minutes ago. He's onboard Air Force Two, listening to Valdivinar and Maximus.

President Carlson forcefully says, "Valdivinar, I heard what you said. You know our position on terrorism. We will not back down or bow down to you or anybody. You've committed war crimes against humanity. You will be arrested and tried in a court of law. All nations, except the Middle East, agree with us. Never has a foreign government ever killed a sitting U.S. President. You will pay the ultimate price, I assure you."

"Who are you?" Valdivinar asks.

"You are speaking to the new President of the United States," he replies.

"Mr. President? Then we weren't responsible for Kennedy's assassination? Are you sure about that?" Valdivinar sarcastically asks. "Look at my mother's wrath," Valdivinar commands, showing a live video of New York City.

At that moment, the city is blown away by several red nuclear missiles. One by one, the large buildings crumble in a cloud of dust. People are running and screaming throughout the streets. Then a large Tsunami begins flooding the city. People drown in the enormous tidal wave. Hovering over the devastation is La Mata Raza. This huge gray serpent-shaped spaceship is launching laser missiles that are causing all the damage. New York City and its people are gone.

Drumpenfeurer, who is in command, comes on the monitor, yelling, "Father, New York City is gone."

"My son, you're doing a wonderful job. Do you see our power, Mr. President?" Valdivinar shouts.

Everyone with Maximus watches on the monitor as New York now lies under the cold Atlantic Ocean.

In frustration, the President shuts off communication with Valdivinar. He asks, "Maximus, how secure is your building?"

"Mr. President, there is no such thing as a secure building anymore. Valdivinar has enough firepower and spaceships to destroy anything at will."

"Okay, I need to be at Washington's Command Center. I can run our defense systems from there," the President says as he walks away from his monitor.

"Mr. Vice President. I mean, Mr. President," Maximus shouts.

The President quickly stops to listen. He turns around and stares at Maximus through the monitor.

Maximus says, "Please give Carol a moment to address the situation. She has vital information you should hear. There may be a possible solution to save lives."

He asks, "Who is Carol?"

"Carol is our secret weapon unknown to all but a few people at NASA."

The President looks up in the air in frustration. "Okay, go ahead," he says politely.

"I'm right here, Mr. President," Carol says.

"Who are you?" the President asks.

"My name is Carol. I'm an advanced supercomputer that analyzes satellite data from Earth and Space. I was created to protect mankind. I'm here to help you. You need to trust me. There isn't much more hope for humans to live on this planet anymore," it urgently counsels him.

"What do you mean, Carol?" The President desperately says, "We are capable of defending ourselves from Valdivinar's forces. I'm on my way right now to launch a direct missile attack. Time is of the essence. We must immediately defend ourselves from this evil threat. You're wasting my time with this mumbo-jumbo talk."

"Mr. President, they possess too many missiles. You will be able to slow them down, but according to my calculations, the world will come to an end. We must begin the evacuation of all people from this planet at once," Carol boldly states.

"What are you talking about? There is no planet habitable in the universe that we know of currently," he says while laughing.

There is a moment of silence in the room. Everyone in the Command Space Center can sense his frustration.

"What are you saying? There *is* such a place?" the President retorts.

"Yes, Mr. President. We have found a planet we call Samra," Carol proclaims.

"Oh my God. Are you serious?" he asks while scratching his head.

"We are dead serious, Mr. President," Maximus replies stoically.

"Well, whatever it takes to save lives. Begin the evacuations and may God be with us. I want a full report on my desk as soon as possible. This is no time to keep any secrets from the White House," the President commands.

Carol replies, "I'm sorry, Mr. President, but the White House has recently been bombed by La Mata Raza spaceship. Everyone in Washington is presumed dead."

The President looks at his monitor showing the White House now blown to smithereens. Everyone at NASA is gasping for air. The newly appointed President looks on in astonishment. He reaches for the missile defense system briefcase, currently handcuffed to the wrist of the Vice-Admiral Alberto Rosario. Precious time has been lost, so the President initiates the Patriot Missile Attack.

After the President and Vice-Admiral enter their secret codes, missiles are launched at missile stations throughout the Middle East and Russia. It is well known to the President that Russia provides the missiles and military strength to bomb the world.

On the monitor, hundreds of explosions are seen in the air. The room is immediately transformed from thoughts of despair to great excitement. They applaud as ally missiles hit their targets. It is amazing to see how quickly the American Missile Defense System can respond. However, considering this small defensive attack, there are many more enemy missile stations they need to eliminate.

"Mr. President, you must negotiate a treaty with Valdivinar to allow all people to evacuate this planet. Now is a good time," Maximus advises on his monitor.

"That I can do. I assure you the treaty will be signed

before the day is done," the President confidently replies.

One hour later, Maximus is in a private room talking to his NASA team about the evacuation plan.

"Please prepare La Azteca for its first launch. Billy, I want the first group of Apaches we've been training here by tomorrow morning ready for takeoff."

"What time, sir?" the young Indigenous engineer asks surprised.

"Have them here at dawn."

"Yes, sir," Billy says excitedly with a smile as he exits.

5

DELIVERANCE

"Walk tall as the trees live as strong as the mountains, be gentle as the spring winds, and keep the summer sun in your heart and the Great Spirit will always be with you."
– Native American Proverb

Fifteen years later, Maximus is on board La Azteca, now hovering over his beautifully built city, El Castillo, on Samra. Melissa designed and engineered this city with Carol's help. The Indigenous human-like natives on the planet are responsible for all the construction.

His eagle-shaped spacecraft was constructed by Boeing in California twenty years ago. This was under unique engineering only Melissa and her husband could design. The spaceship's military intergalactic mission is to evacuate and provide protection for the remaining earthly inhabitants. Even though a treaty has been signed, nuclear warfare continues to kill billions of people on Earth. Maximus, from his command post, is watching through a large window at thousands of refugees disembarking his spacecraft and heading toward the Spaceport terminal.

People enter El Castillo's Spaceport from virtually every

country on Earth. Elvis Presley's greatest hits are playing as they walk inside the building. They are shocked at what they see, but happy to be alive.

"Where are we and where are we going?" a frantic female voice shouts from the crowd.

Carol says on a speaker inside the Spaceport terminal, "Welcome everyone to Planet Samra. Here you will begin your new life. You have all been assigned a new home, clothing and food. There is no need for money because everything is free. Please wear the blue space suit given to you before boarding the shuttles outside the building. Your tour guide on the shuttle will show you the beautiful city of El Castillo. Then you'll be taken to your new home. It's daytime. Our days last 48 hours. All we ask is that you live in peace with each other."

Carol's announcement is repeated in all languages. Everyone temporarily forgets their personal torment and harrowing escape from Earth, so happy are they to be alive.

Chauffeured, rainbow-colored space shuttles are lined up outside the Spaceport with water and bags of food. Each shuttle can carry twenty passengers along with one Apache tour guide. Everyone is taken on a one-hour tour of the big city. Then, they are taken to glass tower condominiums. There are fifty condominium towers in the city. Each has two bedrooms, a kitchen and a spacious living room. Families of five or more are taken to haciendas by an orange-colored ocean.

The city is, indeed, beautiful. Hard yellow clay paves the streets. There is no concrete or asphalt anywhere. From the shuttles, everyone marvels at the colorful landscape and structures. It is well-lit. Light is provided by solar chips made by Melissa. The tour guides share their stories and the history of El Castillo, accompanied by laughter and feelings of joy and tranquility onboard.

Suddenly, another spaceship lands, similar in size to La Azteca. Maximus watches from his ship another five thousand souls walking to the Spaceport terminal. So far, around ten million people have been evacuated from Earth. The evacuations are always dangerous to and from Earth. Zapponata's goal is to obliterate any human who refuses to obey her. She also defies the treaty allowing them to leave Earth.

Drumpenfeurer attacks every spaceship he finds evacuating people. It's not easy to hide from Valdivinar's military forces. They patrol the world with thousands of spaceships at all hours.

A twelve-year-old child named Araceli asks, "What's the name of this place, Grandma?" as they view it from another Mother Ship called The Golden Duck.

Her grandma replies, "It's called Planet Samra. It's going to be our new home, sweetheart. This city is called El Castillo. You can see it has modern domed crystal and gold buildings. Can you see them over there? This place reminds me of Las Vegas. Unfortunately, that city was recently destroyed.

"NASA found this planet with life many years ago after space explorations to Mars, Jupiter and Saturn. Our astronauts lived on Mars for ten years. That's when they discovered this place. They believed it had life. Water, oxygen and gravity are similar to Earth's. The Apache people from New Mexico were the first to live in Samra. They were the brave pioneers of this planet. Fortunately for us, they were able to survive here. Then our President allowed us to come to this New World. He believes we can be happier and safer in Samra. The Samra Space Station and the New World Order was formed by a NASA Space Commander named Maximus Hogan. The New Order is called 'La Libertad.' Some call him the Chief of the Planet."

"Wow, Grandma. The leader is a Native American Chief?" Araceli squeals with delight.

"Yes, that's right. He's the one who saved us from danger," she says as she points to his picture on a brochure in her hand.

She continues reading the brochure to Araceli. "It says that Carol is a supercomputer that helps Chief Maximus. She discovered the Native peoples' DNA from Samra is like ours. They are called Obees. They are cute. They are part human and part droid. Their golden shaggy fur hangs loosely from head to toe. They have two long arms and legs. They are peaceful and technologically advanced in architecture, farming, science, solar energy, and robotics. There are millions of them. They are seven feet tall and work all day long. They constructed the buildings you see down there. Their superior intelligence enables them to speak any language. Chief Maximus had them make farms for our food and these buildings that can withstand the harsh weather conditions on the planet. Look at the huge three-thousand-foot-tall silver towers. Aren't they magnificent? Look at all the beautiful escalators that bridge these buildings. Wow, that's amazing. don't you think?"

She pauses as she takes in the beautiful city. The Mother Ship is about to touchdown on the airfield outside the Spaceport.

Araceli asks, "What else does it say, Grandma?"

She smiles and says, "Look at the car planes flying around us. We're going to get one. Each seats four comfortably and runs on solar batteries. There are large, eagle-shaped battle spaceships to protect us from danger. All battle spaceships are solar-powered and are Chroma Flair painted. That means they change colors based on the reflection of the sun. This is to protect them from enemy invasion. The brightness of these vessels was designed to blind enemy forces while in air combat."

"Grandma, are there a lot of people living here?" Araceli asks.

"There were once over twenty billion people alive on Earth. However, the horrific war has killed most of them. We're lucky to be here, Araceli. Please forget about how awful it was on Earth. We must find our happiness here on Samra, okay? Almost ten million people are living here today."

"Yes, Grandma. I remember all the bombings. That's all I saw when we were there. I don't ever want to go back," Araceli says.

"I don't either," Grandma says as she kisses Araceli on the forehead.

"Grandma, Commander Maximus is my hero," she says with joy.

"He's my hero too. We're alive because of his bravery. In fact, he's the bravest man I've ever known. He risks his life to evacuate people he doesn't know from the evil Zapponata family," Grandma replies with tears flowing down her cheeks.

Maximus is finally relaxing at his beautiful, one-story, five-bedroom hacienda. He can hardly wait for his family to join him. The Samra Space Station is next door. He's on his white leather couch watching Austin Butler's portrayal of Elvis on television. It is mounted on a wall above the white fireplace.

He's reading a book about the centuries of peace between the United States and the world. Historically, world powers manufactured missiles, but they never had to use them. He pauses to think that Zapponata changed everything once Satan gave her the power. However, the United States continued as a democracy. Never has the United States submitted to an autocratic government. All the other countries are now under the rule of a single dictator—Valdivinar. The feud between the United States and Valdivinar has reached its boiling point. Peace has come to an end on Earth. There's only one way out. All people must evacuate to Samra.

Maximus reads these meaningful Native words of wisdom from the book, *The Land Is Sacred*. These words are at the core of our being.

"The land is our mother. The rivers are our blood. Take our land away and we die. What is the good of your stars, trees, the sunrise, and the wind if they are not integral to our daily lives?"

An hour later, Maximus has a vision. One of his spiritual ancestors, Don Francisco, appears before him. He is a six-foot tall famous Yaqui Shaman who guides Maximus through tough times. His skin is a shiny bronze color. He is wearing a black hat and brown robe.

Don Francisco says, "Maximus, the truth about Zapponata is that she sold her soul to Satan when she was twenty-one. In turn, she gave him a son he wanted. He rewarded her with power and control over the world. They believe Magnus is the Great Shaman who will one day take away their power on Earth."

Maximus replies, "We know they want to kill Magnus. However, now we know why. Is there anything else I should know?"

"You must prepare yourself. Death is near you and your family," Don Francisco says as he fades away.

Zapponata is on her balcony sitting on a gray wicker chair. She stares at the large gray buildings as her black spaceplanes fly everywhere. The City of Solorio looks ominous in gray and black. She isn't in a good mood. Grabbing her phone, she calls her son.

"Son, are you there?" she yells.

"Yes, Mother. I'm here in my office in Solorio," Valdivinar answers.

"You must send Drumpenfeurer in La Mata Raza and launch an attack in Japan."

Smilingly he says, "I will do it. When?"

"Tomorrow is New Year's Eve. Make my New Year unforgettable. Anyone who survives our missiles must be found and killed. I want blood," she laughs with joy.

"Yes, Mother. I will do as you command."

His silver tongue had launched his career as a dictator in the Soviet Union for over 20 years. He was exiled to the Middle East. Now, he's in charge of enough military might to destroy the planet ten times over. All missiles were provided through deals made with the United States centuries ago. He immediately calls his evil son on his red and black cell phone.

Drumpenfeurer is in a strip club where he spends most of his life. He's drunk. He's dressed in an orange suit with an orange tie and shoes. His mind is filled with immoral thoughts and beliefs. He has a gift for spreading false information and, in fact, he no longer knows what truth is. His ideology permeates the lives of many throughout the world. He formed a cult, which indoctrinates hate, racism and world armament. Billions of lives have been lost because of him.

Valdivinar says, "We have the green light to launch missiles at the targets we discussed yesterday, son."

"When father?" he asks as he falls off his chair.

"Tomorrow morning at daybreak. We'll invade Japanese stations to take control of their oil, food and weapons."

The next day at 5:00 p.m., many of the major cities in Japan have been destroyed. They leave very few signs of life. The smell of marinating metal, magnesium, aluminum, and titanium permeates the targeted smoldering cities. Fire and smoke fill the large buildings. Cars in the streets are covered in soot. Dismembered bodies are lying on the ground everywhere.

The destruction in Japan is seen from an unknown alien spacecraft hovering ten miles above the surface. The alien vessel is bright silver and shaped like a huge flying saucer. Inside the spaceship, tall Intraterrestrials with long red bodies, thin, elongated legs, cat-like eyes, and gray wings on their backs stare at the devastation caused by La Mata Raza. They are subterranean humanoids. Once, they were celestial angels. However, they were punished and sent to live underground in the center of the Earth before man was created.

The Great Creator speaks to them from a bright light in the sky, "Do not interfere with Satan's work. It is not their time. Go back home."

The largest of the Intraterrestrials answers from the Command Center inside the ship, "Yes, Great Creator."

The twenty Intraterrestrials in the Command Center are disturbed by the horrific site. The entire area lies in smoke and ruin. Humans, animals and plant life are gone.

6

THE BATTLE OF TEARS

Twenty years after Magnus' birth, drumbeats and singing can be heard. There is a Powwow ceremony on the green grass above his parents' bunker home in Silver City. Hundreds of Southwestern Natives in their regalia dance skillfully to the beat of the drum under the warm sunlight. Six Apache men in Levi's and long-sleeved shirts sit around a large drum. They beat the leather-skinned sacred drum as they sing songs. The drumbeat represents the heart of Mother Earth.

Trinidad's father, Golthli, is the only living Apache Shaman healer left on Earth. He will perform a spiritual cleansing of the Earth and her family. Golthli is in light brown pants and a white, long-sleeved shirt with brown moccasins. He is tall and dark with a gold crown and turquoise rock. He is eighty though in excellent health. His white hair falls to his waist.

He can communicate with the spirit world. His spiritual ancestors give him the insight to heal and teach his people. Their message is to take care of the Earth. He has the power to heal people thousands of miles away. Golthli is a world-renowned teacher, healer, warrior, visionary, and wise man. He is also an Army Veteran.

He walks under a large Weeping Willow Tree swaying in the wind. He greets Trinidad, Melissa, Matthew, and Magnus.

Magnus, wearing his colorful Native outfit, is sitting next to Trinidad. She is wearing a long, white dress with embroidered red and yellow roses. They're sitting around a wooden table, eating frybread tacos.

Itza-Chu is now a twenty-seven-year-old man. He's wearing a Native American feathered outfit as he dances with Dahteste in her Native regalia. They've been dancing for twenty minutes.

Golthli takes a special interest in Magnus. He notices his big brown eyes and a huge smile as he eats. He knows Magnus as a young man full of life with innate strength and endurance. He's been raised with a humble heart and taught to respect his elders.

Golthli is alone, praying next to the tree. Magnus walks up to him. He smells the burning gray sage. He touches Golthli's eagle feathers draping his head.

Golthli begins to chant in Athabascan, "Great Creator, I come to you to protect everyone, especially my grandchild, Magnus. Bless this land. Keep us safe from our enemies."

At that moment, he is given a vision of Magnus as a fully grown, muscular man with long, black hair. He's wearing a complete gold Kevlar uniform with a shiny gold helmet that covers his forehead. He is adorned with a dark red cape. His brown eyes can be seen through a glass lens. An image of a black and white Bald Eagle is on the cape. Magnus is sitting in the cockpit of an eagle-shaped, single-pilot blue jet spacecraft. He's chasing the evil villain Drumpenfeurer in a single-pilot black jet spacecraft. They have been in a dogfight for hours above Silver City. Both expertly maneuver in and around the White Apache Mountain. Magnus hits the villain's craft with a purple laser blast. Smoke pours out of the electrical engine. Unknown to Magnus, Drumpenfeurer safely ejects from the cockpit.

Magnus clenches his fists in the air and says, "Take that, Drumpenfeurer."

Drumpenfeurer's spacecraft crashes into the nearby mountain. After flying over his enemy's destroyed vessel a few times, Magnus excitedly says, "You're done, Drumpenfeurer."

Drumpenfeurer, however, is very much alive, and is presently lying on his back on the sandy terrain. He speaks through his wrist phone, "Dad, help me."

Valdivinar is watching his son on the ground from a monitor in his mansion. He answers, "Are you hurt, son?"

He isn't happy with his son because Magnus is still alive.

"Yes," Drumpenfeurer replies as he passes out.

"Okay, someone will be there in ten minutes, son," he says in disappointment.

Golthli felt proud of Magnus' successful battle in his vision. He looks at him with great affection as Magnus turns to look at him, as well.

"I like these feathers, Grandpa. What are they for?" he asks.

"These are sacred Bald Eagle feathers, Magnus. They

protect me from evil spirits," he proudly says.

At that moment, Golthli lifts the mussel shell with the burning gray bundled sage stick. He places the shell on the wooden table. White smoke, smelling of dry sage, fills the air. The smudging of healing and cleansing continues. He takes the stick and gently uses it as a wand to direct the smoke toward Magnus' head. The smudge covers the rest of his brown skin.

He chants in Athabascan, "Wipe away all evil and protect this child forever. Guide his path. Make it straight. Do not let him stumble into temptation."

Trinidad looks at Golthli with pride as he chants and dances proudly to the distant drumbeats. He's welcoming a good life to her son.

Golthli continues, "Great Creator, bless everyone with great wisdom. Bless them to protect our world. Bless them to do great things in life. Bless them to take care of the animals, birds of all kinds, trees, flowers, and all people, for all have spirits that come from you."

He is in a deep trance. Then he hears the sound of the wind talking. He sees a large, gray submarine-shaped Mother Ship flying slowly toward them.

It is La Mata Raza. Inside the ship are several screens monitoring the Powwow. Drumpenfeurer is dressed in an orange suit and tie as he intently watches the Powwow. Women in blue, tight shorts are there to give him support.

"Look at them," he laughs, "They're dancing. How cute. Everyone, standby. We're about to ruin the party."

His assassins, waiting in their fighter spaceships, heard his announcement. Drumpenfeurer is looking at the monitor showing the target.

He stops laughing and announces into his silver

microphone, "Go! No one is to be spared."

And with that, hundreds of small black jet bombers emerge from the Mother Ship. They scatter throughout the bright blue sky. The sky becomes filled with the jet bombers flying overhead. All are single-pilot vessels.

Thousands of armed warriors dressed in brown, white, red, and black feathers with white moccasins are dancing around a large barn fire. Women and children watch the Powwow. The chanting and drumbeats are the heartbeat of the universe. It is believed the reason for the dance is to pray to inspire, preserve and ensure success. Every step is a spiritual prayer to the Great Creator. Dancing with weapons and fighting movements have been used throughout history as a way of training warriors and preparing them emotionally and spiritually for battle. Sometimes, these dances last all night. As the dance continues, the warriors contemplate retaliation for the many dead ancestors who had fought bravely against Drumpenfeurer and his assassins.

Apache Chief Manuelito gets up, raising his clenched hands. Everyone stops and looks at him. No sound is heard but birds screeching and the gusts of wind. Trees are swaying in the wind. His face is painted red and black with a black headband. He is six feet tall with a thin build and a mustache. He points his large black staff toward the eastern sky.

"Look," he proclaims.

Everyone's gaze is upon the enemy vessels coming from the sky on that sunny hot day. Trinidad, who is next to Magnus, watches from her white chair. Everyone turns to Trinidad for guidance. She turns to Golthli who is in deep prayer. The family runs to the bunker for cover. It is just a few minutes away. Trinidad opens the secret underground door and all her family rushes inside.

Carol is heard through the bunker, "It is time. The enemy has come to destroy us all."

Matthew asks, "What should we do?"

"Call the birds and chariots of the air," Carol answers. "Gather all your archers. Prepare your men for a space battle. The assassins are coming full force."

Trinidad runs out of the underground fortress. She points at Chief Manuelito and shouts in Athabascan, "Get your men to the ships. Call the birds and horses of the sky at once."

"Let's go, warriors," the Chief shouts.

He whistles and from the mountains come the flying chariots and War Eagles. Within seconds, there's a loud screech of Bald Eagles in the air. All are soaring toward the awaiting warriors on the ground.

"Get on them," Chief Manuelito yells as they swoop down and land with their heads bowed to the ground. Warriors with painted white faces mount up with laser blasters strapped to their backs.

Loud shouts and whistling are coming from the warriors, "Vamonos muchachos! Today is a good day to die."

Gold-horse chariots are soaring in the air. The white horses are eagerly waiting to go to battle. Thousands of archers are well placed in the White Apache Mountain. They are well hidden from enemy vessels.

Drumpenfeurer's spaceships are within reach of Trinidad's fiery arrows. Hundreds of arrows are fired at once. The sky is on fire. Drumpenfeurer is caught by surprise with this type of attack.

This creates enough distraction for the chariots and Bald Eagles to sneak up on his jet bombers. They fire blue laser blasts from their eyes, destroying several vessels. The chariots are loaded with short-range missiles that take out dozens of

Drumpenfeurer's spaceships.

Trinidad is now watching the battle inside the Command Center. Defense missiles are launched by Cochise. It's a Holy War. There's more noise of bombs blasting than there were on the night Magnus was born. Three monitors explode inside the Command Center. Trinidad is standing with her family by a radio.

She frantically says, "Maximus, Zapponata's men are attacking and I don't think we can take much more."

Maximus demands, "I want all of you here in Samra right now. Your services on Earth are over. All of you must beam to Samra. Take everyone to the transporter chamber room. When you're ready, Carol will beam all of you here."

"No, Maximus. I can't leave our men alone," Trinidad desperately replies.

When she notices the white smoke seeping through the walls, she says, "Maximus, I'm sending our family to Samra right now. Get ready to transport."

He asks, "What about you?"

"You know I must stay and protect our land," she says proudly.

Without hesitation, Trinidad desperately rushes her children, Golthli, Melissa, and Matthew to the transporter room.

"All of you are to go to Samra right now," she demands. "Quickly enter the chamber. Maximus is waiting for you. He'll beam you up to Samra in ten seconds."

The ceiling is collapsing and is now exposed to the smokey sky. No one is willing to leave Trinidad behind.

"Momma, I want to stay with you and fight," Magnus cries.

"No, my son, you must go now. Your father is waiting for

you. Tell him what you've seen. I love all of you so much," she says as she kisses each one.

At that moment, Carol is heard counting down, "Ten, nine, eight, seven, six, five, four, three, two, one."

A white light bathes the family as they vanish from the chamber. Matthew secretly steps out of the chamber without Trinidad noticing.

At that moment, Trinidad sees Drumpenfeurer's vessel one hundred feet above the underground fortress through the hole in the ceiling.

Drumpenfeurer yells, "Trinidad, I found you and your child. Prepare for death."

She responds, "I don't think so. You can't have him. He's going to take you down one day."

She looks at the monitors in the room. The damage is indescribable. Many of her brave men are lying dead on the ground. Several of her aircraft explodes in the air.

Drumpenfeurer's face turns red with anger. He runs to his special red and black tiger-striped single-pilot bomber, the fastest jet bomber in the world. He jumps into the cockpit and fastens his seatbelt, putting on his red helmet. His G10 ship jets out of the Mother Ship and is immediately hit, shaking badly. Smoke is coming from the tail of the craft. He's extremely frightened.

"Keep firing, everyone," he desperately shouts.

Several red laser flashing beams squarely hit NASA's missile base in the White Apache Mountain. It is a significant blast, but NASA's missiles continue to fire back.

Looking at the monitors, Trinidad sees her men taking a beating. Her chariots are motionless on the ground with breathless horses beside them. Even though her white, purple and blue laser blasts fill the air, it isn't enough to overpower the enemy's spaceships. Cochise is doing all he can to fire missiles from the base. NASA's Command Center Room is engulfed in smoke. Several engineers lay dead of asphyxiation.

With sorrow in her heart, Trinidad runs outside the bunker. A small explosion is heard and Trinidad transforms into a superhero. Her outfit is blue and gold. There's a brown and white Bald Eagle embroidered at the center of her purple cape. A gold crown with a turquoise stone adorns her head. She has a pair of gold knee-high boots to complete her magnificent ensemble. Her long beautiful black hair elegantly covers her back. She runs and leaps up to the sky and soars through the air.

As she flies up, she sees Drumpenfeurer in his spaceship. Many loud explosions are seen and heard around them. Both sides have been fearlessly fighting for hours. Eagles are shooting fire from their beaks setting many enemy spacecrafts on fire. Chariots are everywhere shooting beams of blue light laser blasts at the assassin's spaceships. The air is engulfed in battles. The chaos takes its toll on both sides. There is a tremendous cacophony.

Drumpenfeurer speaks from his cockpit radio to his assassins, "This time we're not leaving without killing all of them."

He thinks he's hallucinating as he comes face-to-face with Trinidad the Superhero. "What have we here?" he wonders out loud.

She sees him in his cockpit. He pauses for a minute. He smirks and winks at her before pressing a red missile button. A red ray of light flashes toward her. She moves to the right to avoid it. He sends two more blasts and she avoids both of them. He becomes frustrated so he decides to call for help.

He yells into his radio, "I want all available assassins to

surround the flying woman."

Trinidad is surrounded by twenty assassin spaceships, which proceed to fire red laser beams at her. She's able to deftly weave in and out as she heads toward the mountain.

Frustrated, Drumpenfeurer says, "I'm going to get you, my little pretty. You can't escape the fastest ship ever made."

The chase is on. She's trying to reach the mountain, however, his vessel is too fast. He maneuvers quickly behind her. The chase lasts for thirty minutes. She shoots purple laser blasts from her gold bracelet at him. He shoots back with everything he has. Both avoid impact.

There is still a huge battle being fought by both sides. Chief Manuelito is coming in her direction on his Bald Eagle.

Trinidad is standing on the mountain looking up at Drumpenfeurer's vessel. She shoots a purple laser blast and squarely hits the nose of his ship. He desperately tries to stay away from crashing into the mountain. In a cloud of smoke, he slams into a flat sandy surface a hundred feet from Trinidad. Chief Manuelito sees them both on the ground and rushes toward them.

He says, "How are you, Trinidad?"

She looks at him and then turns to look at Drumpenfeurer. She approaches him, ready for combat. Drumpenfeurer's body is bleeding from his head as he crawls out of the cockpit.

"Tell your men to stop and I'll spare your life," she warns.

"I can't. You will have to finish me," he cries. "My dad will kill me anyway," he lies to her.

Trinidad, feeling compassion for him as a mother, hesitates for a moment. He looks at Chief Manuelito. As she turns to look at Chief Manuelito too, she is struck on the right side of her stomach. A green laser blast from Chief

Manuelito's weapon hits her and she falls to the ground.

"Why?" she asks, looking at him in confusion.

Chief Manuelito turns so that she can't see his face. She gasps for breath. Drumpenfeurer stands up and faces her. She has a clear shot at him. However, before she can point her bracelet at him, she is struck by another green laser squarely on her chest. She's looking up to Heaven as she takes her last breath. Her spirit ascends to Heaven where she joins her ancestors who are waiting to take her to the Spirit World.

"I am now free of this woman," Chief Manuelito brags to Drumpenfeurer.

"Yes, you are. You've chosen to fight for us," he says as he tries to shake his hand.

Chief Manuelito slaps his hand away and says, "I am now a Skinwalker."

"What is that?"

"A person becomes one by killing someone in their family. It is the vilest thing you can do to our people. I did this to possess supernatural powers to transform into a swift-moving animal of my choice. I can wreak a terrible vengeance on all my enemies," he says with great pride.

"Well, I'm glad I'm not your enemy," Drumpenfeurer mumbles.

Chief Manuelito laughs.

An hour later, assassins help Drumpenfeurer board Valdivinar's spacecraft.

"Well done, my son. Chief Manuelito, welcome to your new home. I'm going to make you a legend. You'll oversee our next mission on Planet Samra," Valdivinar says.

"I look forward to serving you. I want to get rid of Maximus and bring back my people," Chief Manuelito replies.

"You will have your people back. You will be a great Chief

for them. I promise," Valdivinar proclaims.

"Mother, can you see the bloody field of bodies, spacecraft, eagles, and horses lying on the ground? The enemy is gone. We will leave this God-forsaken place victorious. Trinidad is dead," he excitedly announces on his spacecraft monitor.

Zapponata is smoking a cigarette in her living room in Solorio. On her wall-mounted monitor, she can see the smoke and remnants of the worse kind of massacre. She sees thousands of dead, bloody bodies and hundreds of animals dead on the dry, sandy ground.

"You've done well, my son. Is the son of Maximus dead?" she asks.

Valdivinar answers, "We are searching for the boy's body, Mother. We still can't find him."

"What? Don't tell me his son is still alive. You fools," Zapponata yells.

7

I Am Chamán

"If we must die, we die defending our rights."
– Sitting Bull

*"It is an unfortunate fact that we can secure peace
only by preparing for war."*
– John F. Kennedy

*"Choose well, my people, because darkness comes and you'll need light
to overcome. The enemy dresses like a deer but kills like a tiger."*
– Native American Proverb

A week after her death, Trinidad's body is laid to rest in a large Native ceremony. All her family is present on an orange hillside overlooking the ocean in Samra. It's a beautiful ceremony with native dancers. Drummers dressed in Native American regalia beat the large drum. Many come to pay their respects. Among them are her children, Maximus, Melissa, and Golthli.

"I promised her that I'd bring her to Samra. It was her wish," Maximus tells everyone with a feeling of great sorrow.

She's buried in a special traditional Apache dress. Her personal belongings are put in her casket, which include her crown, superhero suit, favorite bow, and the tools used for the burial.

Chief Manuelito, who arrived in Samra a few days ago, is observing Maximus and Magnus.

"My sincere condolences to you and your family, my brother," Chief Manuelito tells Maximus.

Maximus looks at him suspiciously. He's thinking about how Chief Manuelito escaped the massacre. Suddenly, a raven screeches loudly from a tree.

"Who did this to my wife?" Maximus asks.

Chief Manuelito cleverly responds, "She was killed by Drumpenfeurer's laser sword. I'm so sorry I wasn't there to defend her. She meant a lot to our people."

Maximus comments solemnly, "Chief Manuelito, choose well, my friend, because darkness comes and you'll need light to overcome it. The enemy dresses like a deer but kills like a tiger."

At that moment, the land shakes tremendously and a thunderous storm takes place. Chief Manuelito uses that disturbance to transform into a gray wolf. He scampers away unnoticed and hides behind a large green and yellow tree. Looking back at everyone, he returns to human form and walks up the seashore alone.

Unscathed by the storm, Golthli is dressed in a white robe with a blue and yellow headband. He has a large eagle feather hanging from his cloak. In his hand are five eagle feathers. With the drum beating and flutes playing, and with sage above his head, he raises a burning mussel shell.

He chants in Athabascan, "Great Creator, thank you for sharing Trinidad with us. Now she has returned to you. She fought many victorious battles against the evil ones. We have become wiser and more knowledgeable because of her. She was a great light who helped us all to see in darkness. Her wisdom made us stronger. We confess that we don't understand why things happen the way they do. We don't know why death comes to our lives so soon. However, we do know that you walk every path of life with us. Remind Trinidad that you are walking with her right now."

The dark orange ocean water is seen in its magnificence as waves hit the shore. It was the same sound Trinidad heard every morning when she lived in Imperial Beach.

"One can think that life is a wave, which in no two consecutive moments of its existence is composed of the same particles," Golthli tells everyone.

As the ceremony ends, everyone is seen walking down the beautiful orange, sloped hill toward La Azteca. Once everyone is aboard, they go to their assigned seats. Maximus and his family are seated in the Command Station Room, looking out the large window. There is much sadness. It is a time to mourn for Trinidad.

Next, the ship's jets blast, quietly lifting it up to the bright orange sky. In a matter of minutes, they're traveling toward El Castillo at a great speed.

One Year Later

It's a cool brisk morning at around six o'clock on Samra. Bright stars are still lighting the sky. Magnus can see a well-lighted coliseum with eagle-shaped starships. They surround hundreds of newly nominated candidates looking for the opportunity to command one of them. He is there with Itza-Chu and Dahteste.

They stand in a straight line, dressed in their assigned blue warrior space suits when a man enters. He is Master Juno, their instructor, an Apache elder. He's dressed in a brown, orange and blue Native outfit, eagle feathers decorating his entire head. From his ears hang silver shell earrings. He has long, white, straight hair. Across his face are red and white painted lines. His appearance is of a bold leader.

Master Juno says, "Welcome, Novatos, to another day of training as future Spaceship Officers. As the prophet Quetzal once said, 'The difference between you and I is I have failed more than you.' What does this mean? It means never giving up. Even if you fail, don't stop. Not all will make it, but those who do will be greatly rewarded. Our mission is to protect our brothers and sisters from the universe of evil. Also, we are the protectors of the land. We are called 'The Brotherhood.' We have been chosen to take care of what our Creator made for us. We believe that almost everything has a live spirit. We are the preservers of life.

"Mother Earth is no longer for us. It is doomed to be destroyed. After all, we didn't do a good job of caring for it. But we still have brothers and sisters who need to be evacuated. Planet Samra is our new home and it will be theirs too. We give our lives to save theirs. We've lived here in peace and prosperity for years. The Natives from this land welcomed us with open arms. We continue to work together as brothers to make this land prosper. The Natives have made our lives better than we ever knew on Earth. There's no need for prisons. There is no illness. There is no hate. There is no discrimination. There is no hunger. There is no homeless. We provide food, shelter and water for all of those in need.

"However, the evil Zapponata wants you back. She is your enemy. Do not be tempted by her propaganda that your life will be great again. Don't be tempted by Valdivinar's eloquent silver-tongued words. They are all lies. Remember the consequences of turning your back on us. We won't condone treasonous acts by our people. Everyone must remain unwaveringly loyal to our New Order.

"As the great Chief Red Jacket once said, 'The Great Spirit has made us all, yet there is a difference between his white and red children; he has given us a different complexion and different customs, a different religion. The Great Spirit does right, he knows what is best for his children; we are satisfied. Brothers, we do not wish to destroy their religion or take it from them; we only want to enjoy our own.'"

Master Juno looks at everyone for a moment and then continues, "If you remember these words when confused by their lies, you will choose wisely. We are who we are and they are who they are. Knowledge of yourself and your enemy makes you stronger."

Ten minutes later, young Magnus, who is now twenty-two years old, is at the center of the arena. He isn't the most liked Novato in the class. Many are jealous because he is the son of Maximus. They take advantage of him because he is a humble and respectful young man.

He whips his black laser stick as he duels ten combatants, each one a few years older than him. Everyone is dressed in purple and black pressurized Kevlar space suits with red headbands. He jumps from side to side and leaps deftly to avoid his opponents' powered laser sticks. Suddenly, he falls to the hard, wooden floor. His large feet keep him off balance most of the time, so he trips over them often.

After a few more falls, Trinidad's spiritual voice is heard.

Magnus pauses to look around for her. Her spiritual image appears to him inside the arena saying in Spanish, "Mi amor, nunca olvides de mi y de tú tierra. Eres el último salvador de nuestra gente. Nunca confies en nadien. Escucha las voces de tús antecedents y tú corazón."

Magnus looks bewildered. He didn't expect to see his mom again. He wonders why she told him that he is the last savior for their people.

He replies, "Mother, I love you so much too. I'll never forget you. I will be a strong savior for our people. I will always listen to my spiritual elders' words of wisdom. I believe in them."

As Magnus is standing motionless listening to his mom's words of wisdom, Master Juno abruptly sneaks up on him from behind and says, "You need much work, Magnus. If you want to become a great Star Ship Officer, you'll need to stay on your feet and not fall so often. That is enough for you today. Vaya a la Cabaña de Sudor por cuatro horas."

As Master Juno points to the sweat lodge door, Magnus walks dejectedly out of the training arena. At the sweat lodge, Magnus is told to disrobe to his shorts.

His bronze, muscular body moves inside the sweat lodge. He is sitting cross-legged around hot stones that are now spewing huge amounts of steam inside the small, pitch-black hut.

The boulders are around twenty-five to fifty centimeters and can retain heat for a long time. They are placed in a pit, which holds the rocks during the ceremony. The hole has been dug in the center of the sweat lodge. Per Native tradition, the hole represents the holiness of the center of the universe. The steam plays an important role in the cleansing of the mind and body. His body is engulfed by the hot, one-hundred-fifty-degree steam. Sweat pours from his flesh before quickly dissipating. The cleansing and purifying is about to begin. Induction of sweating is part of the spiritual ceremony. Prayer, meditation and healing is done by a Native elder.

Golthli enters the hut. Magnus is caught by surprise. He didn't know his grandpa is the Shaman elder in charge of the ceremony.

Magnus listens to his Golthli chant in Athabascan, "Great Spirit, listen to our prayers. We come to you for knowledge and wisdom. Bring courage, wisdom and love to young Magnus. Make him strong and teach him the skills to fight our enemies."

Golthli stops chanting and whisks the steam with a wet, large sagebrush at Magnus. This is the queen of all ceremonial plants. One of the uses of the noble sage incense is to prepare for healing. The smoldering smoke of the plant emits a sensuous odor.

Golthli continues praying to the Great Creator, "Great Spirt, cleanse this space. We are done with the past. Let us find our peace at last. Send your blessings from above with joy and love. As the great Shawnee Chief Tecumseh taught us, the Great Spirit above has appointed this place for us on which to light our fires and remain here."

Magnus feels annoyed and anxious after spending hours in the hot, suffocating hut. However, he begins feeling a sense of euphoria. He's chanting loudly, which makes his Golthli very proud. Magnus is in a trance, talking to his great-grandfather, Tata. He remembers his mom talking about him.

Tata tells him, "I am your Tata, a former Apache Chief. I have been with you since you were born. Listen to me and I will guide you. I will show you signs that will help you during your journey in life. There is much to be done. Trust me because I love you. If you listen, you will help Samra counter any evil threats."

Magnus is confused. "How can I protect everyone on Samra?"

"When you are distressed and confused, meditate and pray to our Great Creator. Let him know you are troubled and seek answers. This is when He will send me to help you. You have the power to heal the sick and injured. I will guide you to victory over evil. You have the power to fly like the birds in the sky. You will win battles over all who are against you and your people. You have the power to transform your body into spirit form and to see the future. You will be able to read people's minds. You now have the power to hear sounds miles away. You are now ten times stronger than any man or beast. You will use these powers to fight for justice. There have been others before you with these gifts. However, they are now in spirit form. I name you Chamán. This is your secret superhero title. Those family members I've chosen will know who you are from this day forward. Promise not to tell anyone your superhero name. Understood?"

Magnus responds, "Yes, Tata. I won't tell anyone."

As he listens to Tata, other spiritual ancestors appear to him. He sees images of his past life who surround him in a deep forest. He's overwhelmed. He can't speak even though he wants to. He is only aware of his breathing and pulse. He gets up to leave the hut.

Golthli dips a sagebrush in water and brushes it on Magnus' face. He then grabs a small piece of sage and gives it to him.

Golthli says, "Magnus, smell the fresh sage and put it behind your ear."

Without hesitation, Magnus does as he is told and, within a minute, he begins to feel like a different man.

"You are chosen by the Great Creator to be the Great Chamán," Golthli proclaims. "You no longer will stumble and fall."

"Really, Grandpa Golthli? My secret name is Chamán? I'm not dreaming?"

"Yes, your Spiritual name is Chamán. You will wear a special space suit to mask your identity."

Golthli knows Magnus has demons inside him. The memory of the loss of his mother still haunts him. However, he believes the memory of his mother's death will strengthen him.

They are still inside the hut. Magnus now sees a vision of many dead Novatos from the Brotherhood on the Samra. It is a vicious battle led by Dictator Valdivinar. There are bloody, mutilated bodies scattered throughout the sandy terrain in El Castillo. Valdivinar is standing over dead bodies with an evil look on his face. He's dressed in a black dojo.

Magnus wakes up from the dream.

"Grandpa, do my dreams have meaning?" he asks.

"Yes, they do. Your dreams will guide your life. Believe in them. They'll keep you from harm and you'll live a good life. Remember that the sky calls to us. There are more galaxies than there are people. Dreams are messages from other worlds. They have great meaning," Golthli wisely replies.

After the sweat lodge ceremony, Magnus and Golthli are standing outside the steaming hut.

Magnus says, "I don't know if I want to be Chamán."

"What do you mean, Magnus?" Golthli asks.

"You are a Shaman with great powers, right?"

"Yes, but that is not all I do. What were you told inside the hut?"

"Tata told me many things about who I am. Is it true that I must save the universe?"

Golthli replies, "Yes, you have been chosen. The Great Creator needs your help to save the universe from evil forces. Much is unknown to us about the universe. Our Planet Earth isn't the only world that is nearing extinction. Many more planets are facing the same problem. Evil forces are everywhere."

"Tata said that I am now Chamán, just like you called me. Who am I to defend the universe from evil forces?" Magnus humbly asks.

"Magnus, it is a great honor to be chosen to be Chamán. There is no reason to be ashamed or scared of the Great Creator's decision. You are very fortunate. Learn to accept it. It is a blessing to help others, don't you think?"

"Yes, Grandpa. I like helping people. How did you become a Shaman, Grandpa?"

"I suffered through the years of a Shaman apprenticeship. There were mandatory teachings before I was allowed to serve as a spiritual functionary in the Apache Tribes. Ultimately, the Spirit itself initiates the Shaman. I found my spiritual forces from my ancestors and they have become a clear channel for my life. This is often referred to as becoming the 'hollow bone.' This means one must expunge all the present fears and past tragedies that haunt them. I must clear the pathway for a Spirit to act in this world. When I perform a healing ceremony, I am not doing the work. I am stepping out of the way. I drop my ego and allow my Spirit to work through me. This level of surrender to the Spirit doesn't come easy to most people. It didn't come easy to me in the beginning. It was the spiritual change itself that was the real initiation."

Magnus looks at Golthli and smiles. He understands his words of wisdom after his experience in the sweat lodge.

The following morning, Magnus is in bed waking up to a new day. He doesn't know if talking to Golthli and Tata at the sweat lodge was all a dream. He's in a white robe as his brother and sister gang up on him. They begin wrestling on the bed like young kids.

Suddenly, Trinidad appears in spirit form. Dahteste and Itza-Chu are shocked and scared. However, Magnus stares at his mom, waiting for her words of wisdom.

"Good morning, my beautiful children," she says. "It's time to rise and shine. It's going to be a wonderful day. It's good to see you again."

"Good morning, Mother," Dahteste and Itza-Chu reply.

"Dahteste and Itza-Chu, I must talk to your brother privately," Trinidad says.

Both walk out of the bedroom through a door that opens automatically by sensing their body heat.

"My son, I have an important message for Chamán," she proudly says.

"Mother, you know Chamán?"

"Yes, I was told by the Great Creator. You have been chosen to protect the universe from evil. You must get to know your powers, my son."

"Yes, Mother," Magnus says half awake.

"Do not trust anyone around you. What you see and hear may not be what's true. I have prayed to the Creator and ancestors to grant you the power to rule over this planet and the universe. Your greatest enemies know you exist. They cannot survive as long as you remain alive. It's time to get up and develop your powers. Let your heart guide your spirit. Your training begins shortly." With that, she smiles and fades away.

Magnus sits sadly on his bed as Maximus enters the room.

His brother shouts from outside, "Hurry up, you lazy bum."

"What's wrong?" his dad asks.

"Dad, they don't want me in the Samra Space Program. I know you're in charge and you want me to become a Space Officer. However, I don't think I'm ready."

"Son, never turn from the old Indian ways you read about. They have been proven for thousands of years. Do not let them die. Learn to be silent because it is more meaningful to our people. Let the speechmakers have their moments. The practice of true politeness allows others to speak. During sorrow, sickness, death, or misfortune of any kind, silence is the mark of wisdom. It's time for you to get going. We'll talk later, Chamán," his dad says proudly.

A huge smile of relief comes across Magnus' face. He jumps out of bed and dresses quickly in his purple uniform.

"Hey, here comes daddy's boy," are the murmurs as Magnus walks down a tunnel of the Samra Training Center. It takes him to a large swimming pool in the Samra Water World Training Facility. Beautiful beams of orange light illuminate the center of the pool. The facility is constructed with a large domed crystal ceiling. An amazing panoramic view of the facility can be seen from above.

Carol announces, "All candidates please report to the swimming pool at Plant 19."

Hundreds of Novatos are in their blue and gray swimsuits. Master Juno is sitting in an elevated blue and gold chair by the pool. He has a gold crown with a turquoise stone in the middle.

He slowly stands and speaks, "Welcome, Novatos, to another day of hand-to-hand combat. Today, you'll demonstrate your ability to fight in water. I want everyone to jump into the pool and begin fighting."

Everyone jumps into the pool, which is twice the size of an Olympic swimming pool. There is a gold underwater steel cave. Next to the pool are fifty steps leading to the top of a fifty-foot volcano spewing steam.

Master Juno mentions, "Only one of you will be crowned victorious after this exercise. The first one to climb to the top of the volcano and dive inside it will be the winner. You may fight until you submit or are knocked out."

Moments later, vicious fighting ensues. Many tap out and watch from the sidelines. Hundreds are seen lying by the pool bleeding after taking blows to the face. Minutes turn to hours as the fighting continues. The loud noise of splashing water and moaning can be heard in and out of the pool. Magnus is one of three left.

Dahteste shouts from outside the sidelines, "You can do it, Magnus. You got this."

Magnus turns to look at her. It is the first time someone is cheering for him. He smiles and turns without hesitation, knocking out another opponent. He sees an opening to the volcano and swims toward it like a shark. He reaches the steps and begins his ascent. A muscular black male Novato reaches out and grabs his leg, spinning Magnus around. He falls back into the pool. His opponent starts to climb the volcano. He's only a few steps from the top. Magnus points with his outstretched arm towards the volcano. Surprisingly, even to him, he begins flying toward it.

Both combatants begin a ferocious wrestling match lasting several minutes. Magnus manages to put a chokehold on him from behind. His speed and know-how of ancient Native fighting dominate the older competitor. His rival falls from the volcano into the pool.

As Magnus climbs to the top, a loud jeer from his peers rings out. Everyone is mystified. The Novatos and Master Juno wonder how he could fly and beat the older and stronger foe.

"He's cheating," the Novatos shout.

He's now standing at the top of the volcano. He looks down at the center of the shaft. Hot steam obscures his vision. He can't see the water.

"Jump, jump, jump," his fellow contestants shout as he stands motionless.

Just then, Tata appears to Magnus and says, "I'm so proud of you, Chamán. Jump and don't be afraid. The Great Spirit will carry you to safety. Trust your heart."

"Thank you, Tata," Magnus says, feeling more confident.

He takes a deep breath and dives into the volcano. Minutes later, his eyes open to see Master Juno standing over him with Maximus.

"Good job, son," his dad says with a smile.

He grabs his arm and lifts him to his feet. The loud noise of clapping and jeers fill the center. Master Juno presents him with a gold laser saber.

Master Juno says, "This competition earns you the right to become the Commander of Thumbelina, our great Mother Ship. She's one of our largest Mother Ships that control the universe."

At that moment, everyone looks up at the two hundred foot, rainbow-colored, eagle-shaped vessel hovering above the crystal-domed ceiling. The shiny silver and purple changes colors from the sun's reflection—perfect for blinding the enemy in flight.

Magnus turns around and faces his fellow Novatos.

Some cheer and others chant, "Cheater, cheater."

He stands in front of everyone feeling like the greatest person on the planet. It is a dream come true. The jeers don't bother him anymore. He is Chamán.

Magnus says, "Thank you, Master Juno."

He notices a large, familiar male figure in the middle of the crowd. He turns and looks at his dad in astonishment.

"Is that Cochise?"

His dad nods his head. Magnus is glad to see him. Cochise just arrived at Samra yesterday.

Magnus runs to him. It feels like he's running in slow motion. He's bumping into others but desperately trying to get to him. It seems like an eternity. They hug each other.

The tall robot says, "I missed you, Magnus."

"I missed you more, but I thought you were dead. How did you get here, Cochise?"

He stops hugging him and says, "Magnus, you are so big and strong. Congratulations. You remind me of your father and mother. Thanks to your father, I am here. He is saving many from Earth. The land and people are dying over there. People can't survive without your father's help. Maximus delivers food and water for many who are still waiting to migrate to Samra. He found a way to sneak me here. It is pure genius and a miracle that I am here. We were hiding all this time in the copper mines in Santa Fe, New Mexico. Nobody bothered looking inside the mines because they heard they were cursed. For thousands of years, there were stories of underground humanoids living inside the mines. No one who came near them ever returned. It's believed by our people that there is life under the surface of the Earth. They were the first to live on the planet. The Intraterrestrials were punished by the Great Creator for things they did to His people. They once were angels. However, they had babies with women, which was against His will. They protected us from nuclear missiles. Discreetly, they came out of the Earth to nurture and comfort us. We never saw what they looked like."

"Did they take care of everyone?" Magnus asks.

"It was difficult caring for everyone. However, to Intraterrestrials, it was easy," Cochise answers.

"What are they called? Did they ever speak to you?"

"Our people call them Niños de la Tierra—Children of the Earth. No, they never spoke to us. However, they used telepathy and clairvoyance to understand us. They can also hypnotize humans to forget what they heard or saw."

"Thank you for telling me about them. They may be of help in the future," Magnus says.

"Enough of the past. How are you doing here? I am told you are Chamán," Cochise says as he looks around.

"Yes, I've been told by the spirit world that I am now Chamán, the savior of the universe," he jokingly says.

Cochise looks at him sternly. He turns and walks away from him.

"What's wrong?" Magnus asks.

Cochise stops and turns around to face Magnus and asks, "Who told you, my boy?"

"Tata. Is that important?"

"Yes, it is. Tata is very important in your life. It would help if you did not offend our ancestors. There have only been five Chamáns before you. That is a sacred name. Has anyone told you?"

"No," Magnus admits, "I believe I am to protect our people from the evil in the universe, right?"

"You must prepare yourself, Magnus. First, you are to dedicate your life to fighting for justice. Second, you will hunt down and eliminate all those who harm others. Have you tried your powers?"

"Well, I just flew out of the pool. I didn't know I could do that," he said with a smile.

"You have special powers that you need to discover. You will learn to use them. We will teach you how to become a great warrior and healer," Cochise advises.

"Should I stop training with Master Juno?"

"Why do you ask that, Magnus? Do you not like it here?" Cochise asks in confusion.

"I feel I don't belong here. No matter what I do, nobody likes me."

"Don't concern yourself with what you see and hear. Trust your spiritual instincts; they'll take you far in life. You have special powers that you need to develop. Learn to live your life through the powers of your spiritual ancestors who are always with you. They will guide you on your journey. There is something you need to know about yourself," Cochise says mysteriously.

"What?" Magnus curiously asks.

"You are the only hope for our people. Without you, our universe will be overrun by the evil forces of Satan, who we call the Evil Spirit."

"Thank you, my brother. I am excited to begin. I will do all I can to protect the universe," Magnus says as they both walk out of the facility.

"Golthli and I will be waiting for you at his house at sunrise tomorrow," Cochise says.

The following day, Magnus secretly leaves his home. He's wearing Native brown pants and no shirt. His long, black, shiny hair is bound with a gold headband, in the middle of which is a shiny amethyst stone. He's running through a colorful yellow, green, orange, and pink forest. It is filled with chirping bluebirds, snorting elephants, roaring lions, and grunting chimpanzees.

The sun is coming up in the west. The sky is a beautiful bright orange. There are no clouds. It is around ten degrees Celsius. Joining him is a beautiful black and white colobus monkey, full of life and energy. He jumps on Magnus' shoulder.

"Who are you?" Magnus asks in surprise.

"Master, my name is Milo. Your Grandpa Golthli has given me instructions to take care of you. I know you are Chamán. I'll be teaching you about life on this planet. Also, I have learned about the history of the planet called Earth. We have much to talk about."

Magnus hears a noise. He turns and, from behind a tree, Cochise and Golthli appear in brown leather Native American-style pants and moccasins with no shirt. Both have a gold headband with a turquoise stone.

Golthli says, "I'm happy you met Milo."

He signals with two fingers for Magnus to follow. They walk through the beautiful large trees. After five minutes, they come to a small hut—an inipi, just like the one at the Samra Space Training Center. Magnus feels a sudden surge of adrenaline.

All three are inside the sweat lodge watching the glow of white and purple sparks glistening on the large, hot, egg-shaped boulders.

"That's a good sign, Chamán. The sparks mean our

ancestors are pleased that you're here with us today. They know you have come to learn about your powerful skills. You're here for spiritual knowledge. Is this true?" Golthli asks.

"Yes, Grandpa. I come with the willingness to learn about becoming Chamán," he respectfully tells him.

A strange voice comes from Golthli's mouth, "My son, this will be your spiritual journey to become Chamán. Your ancestors will bring you surprising teachings. Be strong. Be decisive. Be fully responsible for your actions. You have the body of a man. However, you are not to think like a man. The great sin is to believe that life itself is not good. You will be responsible for bringing justice to a universe struggling for survival. You must bring dignity in the face of violence and social injustice. This will be a remarkable journey. These are the first awesome steps to becoming a Chamán with great powers.

"You will live as a person traveling on paths that have heart. There, you will travel. The only worthwhile challenge is to traverse its full length, which you will learn in due course. Here, smoke this."

Chamán takes two puffs from a long, brown, wooden pipe.

"This is for meditation with the other world. The plant is of the Deer God. It'll open the channels of communication with your ancestors. It is a sacred plant. It is always to be treated with respect. If smoking is done incorrectly, it could cause harm to you. The plant will punish you and treat you badly."

Golthli adds, "A Chamán goes to knowledge as he goes to war. He is wide awake. He is fearless. He reacts with respect and courage. Going to knowledge or going to war in any other manner is a mistake. He will live to regret his steps."

Chamán is in a deep trance. He sees figures of men around him, Tata among them. They are all Native American Chiefs. It's mysterious and somehow frightening to him. He's fighting to survive this ritual enlightenment.

The strange voice continues from Golthli's mouth, "These are your allies. They will bring you power. They will serve as your advisors. View the world as energy. Look at yourself as a luminous egg that gets its light from the assemblage point of awareness. This is located in the heart. A man does not have counterparts for all emanations. He cannot be aware of everything outside his energetic field. However, as a Chamán, you can move and shift the assemblage point. This will make you aware of more of the world—both within and without. The 'ally' is a powerful spirit. It can come to life to help advise.

"The ally will give you the strength necessary to perform acts, whether big or small, right or wrong. The 'helper' is there to enhance your life and will guide your movement. He will enhance your knowledge and will enlighten you to see things that are beyond man's understanding.

"You can achieve this insight as a Chamán. You will discover many secrets of reality through your 'dream body.' Learn to engage in this practice of dreaming. Learn to move between worlds during the day. I now give you all the power of Chamán's knowledge. You have been given supernatural powers to fight all evil in the universe. Beware! What I have given you can make you miserable or it can make you strong. A path is only a path. There is no guarantee. You can drop out if that is what your heart tells you. However, look at every path closely and deliberately. Try it as many times as you think necessary. Then ask yourself, does the path have a heart? If it does, the path is good; if it doesn't, it is useless. Remember, the basic difference between an ordinary man and you is that you take everything as a challenge. The ordinary man takes everything as a blessing or curse."

Five minutes later, Chamán is awake and hears Golthli announce in his Native Athabascan language, "You are now a Denali." It means 'The Great One.'

"Tsin'aen," Chamán responds in Athabascan.

As the steam from Chamán's body rises to the Heavens outside the sweat lodge, Milo jumps on Chamán's head. They walk with Cochise and Golthli toward a beautiful house. It is made of natural stone-tanned walls. Large green and yellow parrots are chirping. The wind is cool and refreshing. Magnus feels like himself again. All three walk inside the house. Magnus showers and puts on loose purple clothing. He prepares for the next lesson.

After running for two hours through the magnificent rainbow forest, Magnus is showing no signs of exhaustion.

Heavy, brown, half-ton boulders surround the house. Golthli has him make one pile of boulders in front of his Hacienda-style home. Magnus begins to lift them one by one on his shoulder. Once the pile is done in five minutes, Golthli and Cochise look at it in amazement.

"Very nice, Magnus. You have great strength and stamina for combat. Now, we will train you to fight like a warrior," Cochise says.

He begins to teach Magnus the skill of the chokehold from behind the back. They practice for hours in the front yard.

"Now, we will engage in laser combat. Take your laser sword," Golthli commands.

Cochise holds his blue laser with both hands. Magnus

turns it on and it begins to flash. They press a button on their swords to set them for a non-fatal blow. Both are weaving and dodging each other's laser. It's a magnificent show of talent by both combatants. Finally, Magnus stuns Cochise, dropping him to his knees.

"Great work, my brother. You are ready," Cochise says.

Magnus helps Cochise to his feet.

Cochise says with a smile, "Great job, brother. No one has ever beaten me."

Magnus is inside a room, changing into his regular Native American clothes. He sees Cochise and Golthli walking in his direction. In Cochise's big hands is a shiny gold Kevlar suit with a gold helmet and red cape. He really likes the purple shiny knee-high boots.

Cochise says, "This is made for Chamán."

"Really? Who made it?"

"The space suit was made by your mother."

"How did she know?" Magnus asks in confusion.

"You didn't know this about your mother, but she was a Chamana. She had the same superpowers you now have," he solemnly says.

"Wow, my mom was a Chamana," Magnus expresses with a huge smile on his face. "That is amazing. I always thought she kept a deep secret from us."

He excitedly looks at his superhero suit and begins to put it on. However, he has trouble slipping into it.

"Can you help me?"

Cochise laughs and tells him, "Magnus, I want you to say the magic word, 'Misty.'"

"Misty?" he asks, bewildered.

As Magnus says the word, he is transformed into Chamán. He has his superhero Kevlar uniform on.

"Wow, you guys are full of surprises," he says in a deep, strong voice.

There's a brown, white and green Bald Eagle on the backside of the cape. The light steel wardrobe is laser-blast-proof. It is something he has never seen before. His helmet is adorned with a gold crown and a turquoise stone. The high collar makes him feel cool. He is totally amazed.

"When you need it, all you have to do is call for it by name. It'll track your location by an embedded GPS device. It'll be like calling your horse," Golthli said laughing.

"Thank you. I feel like a completely different person."

"One day, we will be thanking you," Golthli responds. "Now, the next lesson will be for you and your spacesuit to become one. You're going to fly to the big mountain and back. The suit will take off when you say, 'Let's go,'" Golthli instructs.

"Let's go," Chamán says as he raises his right hand with a clenched fist at the mountain.

He is caught by surprise with the speed. He twirls awkwardly around in circles and almost crashes into a blue and white bird.

"Sorry," he says to the bird. His outstretched fist keeps him headed in the right direction.

"Can I do it again?" he asks.

They both laugh and say, "Of course. Do it as many times as you wish."

He is off again, achieving greater speed with each blastoff.

"So, I just have to say, 'Misty?'" he asks after finishing the lesson.

"Yes, my son. That's all you have to do. You now have the power no one has ever been given. Our Great Creator said that from our people will come a Great Chamán with superpowers beyond our imagination. But remember—with great power comes great responsibility," Golthli tells him smiling proudly.

8

BATTLE OF SAMRA

"All my warriors were brave and knew no fear. The soldiers who were all killed were brave men too, but they had no chance to fight or run away…We did not go out of our own country to kill them. They came to kill us and got killed themselves."
– Sitting Bull

The following day, Chamán joins Golthli and Cochise at the Samra Space Training Center. They board Thumbelina. Chamán is observing all the electronic components inside the Command Post which are currently transmitting live information.

Carol says, "Welcome aboard Golthli, Cochise and Chamán. The training will begin shortly. The service and payload modules are functioning properly."

Chamán's superhero suit shines inside the Command Post light. His red cape with the golden eagle hanging down his muscular back is noticed by the crew standing in the room.

"Are you ready to take her for a test run?" Golthli asks.

"Of course? Let's do this. When do I start?" Chamán asks.

"Chamán, power her up. Press that green button and then the blue one for lift-off," Golthli directs as he watches him closely.

Thumbelina makes a jet rocket sound. They can feel the vibration of the vessel lifting off the ground. Suddenly, it shakes and an alarm goes off. They leave it to Chamán to figure it out. He looks to them for answers. However, they blankly stare at him. He's in a panic but understands this is another lesson. He has studied the operation manual for almost a year and has memorized it.

"Okay, the quadruple-delta wings must be energized," Chamán tells himself.

He looks for the lever near the control board. He presses it and lifts it gently to forty-five degrees. The loud alarm ceases and they are safely in the air. It is an amazing sight for Chamán to see all the battleships protecting the homeland, as he stares out the large vessel's window. Hundreds of space cars whisk by Thumbelina.

"We want to go to Planet Zemplar, two hours away. Please set the coordinates to longitude one-hundred-eighty degrees and forty degrees latitude," Golthli commands.

Chamán sets the coordinates and Thumbelina zooms toward Zemplar. He presses the white button to energize the ship's 'sling shot effect.' This maneuver speeds space travel.

A white streak of light is seen on the tail end of the spacecraft. Chamán is ecstatic. This is an unbelievable moment for him. He looks confidently out the large window as they approach Zemplar.

"Prepare to land, Chamán," Golthli says with a smile.

Luckily, Chamán remembers what he's read about landing instructions. His photographic memory comes in handy and the ship lands without a hitch. With Milo on his shoulder during the entire trip, Chamán is living the dream on board his amazing starship.

Chamán, Milo, Golthli, and Cochise head toward the Transporter Room to beam themselves down to Zemplar. They are standing there looking at the sandy and windy terrain. The area is desolate. Even though there is life on this planet, none can be seen.

One hour later, onboard Thumbelina, they are going back to Samra. Chamán stands inside the Command Post. Looking out the window, he notices hundreds of strange vessels heading toward El Castillo.

Carol announces, "The enemy found a way through our electromagnetic force field."

"Who are they?" asks Chamán.

"It is Drumpenfeurer and his assassins from Planet Earth. They breached our two hyperspace corridors—from Samra's moon and the other on Planet Uran. The hyperspace corridors are supposed to generate an electromagnetic field to prevent intruders from compromising a pathway into Samra's atmosphere."

Watching above Samra, Maximus is inside La Azteca. He calls to Carol from his wrist phone, "Our satellites are picking up communications from Drumpenfeurer and his assassins. They found a pathway into our stratosphere. Bombing has begun here in El Castillo. We are fighting back."

"Alert all men that this is an epic invasion," Carol announces on the intercom. "All alliances must be advised. Maximus, you need to get Cisco's team at once. Your Novatos and the Samra Native Obees need to be positioned on the ground. Put the Eagle Ships in the air with Master Juno leading them."

On Maximus' screen appears a large, dark Native male,

General Chuatemoc. He sits by his radio in his hacienda-style home. He's in charge of the city of Zapopán a hundred miles west of El Castillo. He has long black hair. Green army fatigues cover his body from head to toe. His eyes are jet blue.

"General Chuatemoc, we're being attacked by Drumpenfeurer's assassins," Maximus says. "Right now, maintain your men's position in Zapopán. I might need your help. I'll let you know."

Then, in a strong voice, General Chuatemoc says, "I want Drumpenfeurer. I lost my family and many warriors to that scumbag. They broke the treaty they signed with President Carlson, right?"

"Yes, Zapponata has broken another treaty like hundreds of others broken on Turtle Island."

"We're here if you need our help, sir."

"Thank you, my friend," Maximus replies as he presses another button on his computer.

A gorgeous Native American Apache woman appears on his screen. She's wearing a beautiful red, green and white Native dress with an eagle feather hanging from her long, ponytailed, blonde hair. She's hundreds of miles away in the city of Zoey. Drumbeats are heard in the background.

"Commander Zoey, come in, over," Maximus says over the radio.

"How can I help you, my dear?" she answers with a smile. It is well known she has a crush on him.

"Commander Zoey, we're under attack by Zapponata's evil space force," he replies as loud bombs are heard in El Castillo.

"Maximus, they found a way to infiltrate your electromagnetic fields? They are a true nuisance to us," she replies with concern.

She had been evacuated from Earth years ago, by Maximus, who saved her life in Douglas, Arizona. Extremely intelligent and quick-witted, she is now in command of the north side of El Castillo. The city is named after her. Attacks by invaders aren't new to them. Maximus and Commander Zoey fought together in a dozen similar battles with extraterrestrials that come from different planets in the universe.

"What would you like us to do this time, my friend?" Commander Zoey asks calmly.

"I need you to send your best space commander and attack them from the north side of El Castillo. We can hold them off until your army arrives," he tells her persuasively as bombs continue to explode.

She presses her wrist cell phone. "Cisco, come in over," she urgently utters.

"This is Cisco, Commander Zoey," a strong masculine voice replies. He is a fearless Apache Spacefighter who commands Zoey's Mother Ship, La Victoria.

She says, "Hey dude, I need you to load your army on your battleship ASAP. Chief Maximus needs your help defending the north side of El Castillo. They're under attack by Zapponata's assassins."

"Commander Zoey, we're already onboard La Victoria kicking back and waiting for action. Tell him we'll be there in five minutes," he confidently replies as he sits inside his Command Post.

"They'll be there in a few minutes, Maximus," Commander Zoey quickly tells him.

"Thank you, Commander Zoey. I owe you one. Over and out," Maximus graciously says as he presses another button on his computer.

There are hundreds of Commander Zoey's small single-pilot jet bomber vessels above El Castillo, piloted by Apache Novatos from her Space Force. They're dressed in purple combat fatigues. Gas masks cover their faces. Only their eyes and part of their hair can be seen. Their vessels are rainbow-colored and blind the enemy. As they quickly engage the assassin's crafts, their blue laser lights catch the enemy by surprise. At least twenty enemy spacecraft are immediately destroyed. The damaged vessels fall to the rough, sandy terrain and crash.

Cisco shouts on his radio, "Z10, keep to the left. You have two dingers above you. Turn right and go up behind them."

Z10 says, "I'm on him, Cisco."

He makes the moves and blasts the assassin's craft from the orange skyline.

"Great job. Now you have five more on your flank," Cisco warns.

Cisco fires purple lasers from La Victoria, destroying the five enemy spacecraft instantly. His numerous victories have made him a legend on Samra.

"We'll land in five minutes," Cisco orders from his Command Post. "Looks like they need our help on the ground. Prepare to land and attack with all you've got, my brothers."

He is now inside his rainbow-colored, single-pilot, eagle-shaped jet bomber. He's chasing assassins' spacecraft, blowing away each one in his path. The battle in the air lasts around thirty minutes. Suddenly, Cisco's vessel is hit by a red laser and smoke emerges from the left wing. His space jet begins to shake and he's losing control. He smashes into a sand dune.

Cisco is on the ground, motionless. His left hand begins

to move. Life is slowly coming back to his large body. One eye opens. The emerging determination of the experienced warrior's fighting spirit can be seen. He leaps to his feet and starts engaging in laser saber combat. His expertise with his purple laser wand kills hundreds of assassins and droids. He is almost supernatural in his movements, flying side to side, up and down, and several feet up to escape death.

Drumpenfeurer's army, dressed in black and orange, is strong and has skillful fighters. However, they are taking a beating as they are no match for Cisco and his fierce Apache Warriors. Their faces are painted with two white lines and eagle feathers on their heads. Master Juno's Novatos are fighting on the ground in white and silver army fatigues with white bandanas.

After hours of red, white and purple laser beams filling the air, now silence and peace reign. The battle is over. The Novatos and allies successfully defend El Castillo.

They raise their fists and shout, "We won."

Drumpenfeurer is seen in La Mata Raza. He leaves the rest of his men behind to escape.

He's yelling at everyone inside the ship, "What happened? Why can't anyone fight like them?"

Valdivinar is watching him from his home in Solorio and says, "Son, did you kill Maximus' son?"

"Father, they killed most of our men. I never saw him. I'm coming home," he replies as sweat trickles down his forehead.

"Son, we are in big trouble," he exclaims, then lowers his head wondering how his mother will take the news.

Meanwhile, Chamán, Cochise and Golthli witnessed the

whole battle from the Command Post onboard Thumbelina.

Chamán asks, "Who is that Apache Warrior who killed hundreds of assassins?"

"He is known as the greatest fighter in the galaxy. His name is Cisco. He's your mom's only living brother," Cochise says.

Chamán is amazed that Cisco is his uncle. Things are beginning to make more sense about where he gets his superpowers.

"Grandpa, does he have the same powers as me?" Chamán inquires.

"Yes and no. He is highly skilled with similar talents. However, they do not compare to yours," Golthli responds.

As Chamán lands the spacecraft near the field of dead bodies, he is led by Golthli to some of the Novatos who are barely alive.

Chamán kneels and raises his arms, asking the bleeding Novato warrior, "Where is it hurting, my brother?"

The Novato looks at him with his red bloodshot eyes and stutters, "My upper legs were both lasered. The pain is unbearable. Please help me."

Chamán is now in a trance and chanting. He allows his spirit great-grandfather, Tata, to heal the warrior.

"Get up," Chamán commands the Novato.

The Novato stands and others are astonished that he is healed. He thanks him and runs to let everyone know that Chamán saved his life. Chamán continues to heal more wounded through his Tata.

Hours later, Master Juno is seen saluting his men from the Samra Training Station platform, proclaiming victory over Drumpenfeurer's assassins. His face is lined with red paint. He raises his flashing, gold light laser saber above his head.

All Novatos do the same and shout, "Long live Samra…long live Samra."

They have fought many battles against invaders. However, this battle is different since it is the first attack from their homeland enemy.

"You idiot," Zapponata yells at Drumpenfeurer as she appears to him on a monitor inside La Mata Raza's Command Post. "What will you do now? You are of no use to me if you can't kill that boy and bring my children home. Don't you understand that we'll die if he lives?"

In her dark bedroom, she throws her black wooden cane across the room and falls to her knees crying.

9

THE RIVALRY

"Two wolves are fighting inside all of us. The first one is Evil, and the second is Good…which wolf will win? The one you feed."
– Native American Proverb

The following morning, Trinidad appears in Magnus' bedroom. He is awakened by the sunlight and noise of vessels patrolling El Castillo. Itza-Chu and Dahteste are wrestling on the floor.

"Give up?" Itza-Chu says as he pins her to the floor.

She screams, "Never, never."

At that moment, Dahteste twists her body. She wraps her legs around his stomach. With her arms, she's choking his neck from behind. He falls to the floor. In seconds, he taps her arm in surrender.

"My children, I'm so happy to see all of you again," Trinidad proudly says.

"We're just as happy to see you. We miss you so much, Momma," Dahteste replies.

"Yes, Momma, we're so happy you have come to be with us," Itza-Chu chimes in.

"I have been given a new life to watch over you and your father by the Great Spirit. I'll never leave you."

Magnus says, "I hope you never leave us."

"That is so sweet of you. I will tell you one thing, I am always watching over you," Trinidad says with a big smile.

"Look, it's our S3000 battleship flying over us," shouts Itza-Chu, as he and the others look out the window.

"I'm going to fly one of them someday. I want to fly and command the universe in one of them," he continues.

"Sure you are, brother. But first, you need to show Master Juno you can fly it," Magnus joshes.

Dahteste replies, "I bet I'll beat both of you dreamers to fly in one of those vessels."

"My children, I love your spirit. I have a message of wisdom for you today," Trinidad says, looking at each of them with a motherly smile.

"Please tell us, Momma," Dahteste implores.

"Please remember that history is not there for you to like or dislike. It is there for you to learn from. And if it offends you, even better. Then you are less likely to repeat it. It's yours to erase or destroy."

Itza-Chu, who was happy at the outset, is now upset after hearing his mother's words. He covers his ears with both hands.

"What's wrong, Itza-Chu?" Trinadad asks.

"Momma, why do you speak to us that way?" he remarks sharply.

"I don't know the future for each of you and the journey each of you will choose," she wisely says. "Just remember that no matter what happens in your life, you must always love each other no matter what."

"Momma, there are many things I agree and disagree with

here on Samra," Itza-Chu remarks. "Even though our father has brought peace and prosperity to everyone, I am not sure it'll last forever. I see and hear some are not happy with this type of life. They aren't satisfied. Many want to go back to Earth."

"My son, happiness is very complex, and each person has strengths and weaknesses. Above all, we have been given the absolute power of 'free will' to make choices. Your father created a new form of World Order that gives to those who don't have. This is from our Native roots as Apache people," Trinidad explains. "Before the Europeans came to Turtle Island, we had no prisons. They weren't necessary. When someone needed food, clothing or shelter, our people provided it. There were no homeless people in that world. There was no need to commit crimes. Your father has created a world similar to what it used to be like on Earth for the Apache people. This is what he calls 'Making Life Great Again.'

"Look around El Castillo. We have free space cars and homes here in Samra. We have professional sports teams for baseball, football, basketball, tennis, and swimming. We have horse racing. People can go anywhere on this planet without any fear. Your father has created a modern civilization on this planet. There's enough food for everyone. There are no bills we must pay. To heal the sick, we use natural herbal remedies, which grow freely in the ground. Our ancestors used them for thousands of years and lived much longer than most, especially during the last years when the Earth was polluted with toxic gases. We have no extravagant healthcare plans to pay for drugs.

"I know you read what Luther Standing Bear once said, 'Mother Earth has given us strength and health.' You also read what Lorraine Canoe once said, 'The Earth supports our feet as she is instructed. The women and Mother Earth are one—givers of life. We are her color, her flesh and her roots. Once we acknowledge and respect her role, a true relationship begins. All that is from her returns to her: the plant life, the medicine plants, the strawberries, the three sisters, corn, beans, and squash, and the bodies of water. It is good for the skin to touch the Earth. The old people liked to remove their moccasins and walk with bare feet on the sacred Earth. It was the final abiding place of all things that lived and grew. The soil has powers to soothe, strengthen, cleanse, and heal.'

"Hatred has grown stronger after years of defiance by other worlds. You've seen this. Always remember to choose to be part of your father's legacy. He is the Chief of Planet Samra. As you saw yesterday, he defeated the evil forces of Drumpenfeurer's assassins."

"Momma, but Drumpenfeurer escaped and will be back. I know what he did to you. I want to destroy him," Itza Chu responds.

"His family's reign will not last. Their empire will not prevail. Even though what you feel is understandable, revenge only comes from immoral beliefs. Our Creator does not condone it. It will only lead to repeating the history that Mother Earth has to bear. Earth is being destroyed. Evil forces take her natural minerals, trees and animals to support an egotistical way of living. We fight them, but their laws protect their corruption. Always remember, we have been blessed with a second chance. We can save not only this planet but also Mother Earth. Hold fast to what our Creator and ancestors have given to you. Do not let them down. Take care of this planet. Protect it with your life."

"All candidates, please report to the coliseum," Carol

announces over the intercom in the room.

"Did you hear that?" Dahteste asks.

"Go my children. Do the Lord's work," Trinidad says as she fades from the room.

All three jump with excitement and rush to get ready. Itza-Chu, who is long-limbed, was able to rush out first. All three are dashing down the rugged terrain toward the Samra Training Center Coliseum.

"We should have left you home with Momma. You're too young for any of this. You won't last two hours," Itza-Chu scolds Magnus in the locker room as everyone puts on their uniform.

"I'll last here longer than you, brother. I'll show you," Magnus answers confidently.

Master Juno is listening as he enters the locker room. He's wearing a brown, Native American outfit with long feathered earrings.

"Isn't that true, Master Juno?" asks Itza-Chu.

Master Juno shakes his head and says, "Of course, you're old enough, Magnus, to participate."

Magnus feels everyone staring at him. He thinks they are looking for signs of weakness. He stands and walks out to the coliseum. Half an hour later, all are in a line facing a large stage where Master Juno stands tall. It is cold enough to see everyone's breath.

Master Juno announces, "Today's exercise will be man-to-man combat. Everyone will be matched with an opponent. You will engage in tomahawk laser fighting. Each tomahawk laser is set to give off a two-amp shock charge. If you are hit five times, you're out. Select an opponent."

Everyone in the coliseum chooses an opponent and takes up a tomahawk laser.

Master Juno shouts, "Begin."

Magnus is struggling with his tomahawk laser. Master Juno is watching. Several charges from his opponent's tomahawk stun his arms and legs.

"Magnus, come here," Master Juno says.

"Yes, Master Juno."

"Close your eyes and let your heart guide you. Flow with the energy of your weapon. See your opponent's tomahawk light and attack it swiftly. Trust your heart. Be one with your weapon. Let it do its work. Trust it. Your energy should flow through it. It'll target your opponent's weaknesses," he explains as he covers Magnus' eyes with a red bandana.

Magnus is seen blocking laser shots in every direction. He pressures his opponents into submission, striking them repeatedly. He's listening to his heart. His ability is far superior to his peers. When he takes off his bandana, he finds that he is the only one remaining. Everyone again is overwhelmed by the skill he displays.

Master Juno raises his hand in victory. Everyone is astonished. His dominating display of using the laser tomahawk was impeccable.

Itza-Chu is seen walking away from the outdoor arena in anger. Magnus acknowledges everyone's applause and cheers. He watches his disgruntled brother walking out of the coliseum alone. Dahteste notices the same thing and rushes to try and comfort him.

"Brother, what's wrong?" she asks.

"Leave me alone, Dahteste. I have to go home. I have some things to do by myself," Itza-Chu angrily says.

"Can I come with you?"

"No, I said I need to do these things on my own," he reiterates.

"Okay. I'll see you later at the baseball game, okay?"

"Sure," he says trying to avoid her.

She runs back to the arena to celebrate her brother's victory, hugging Magnus to the point of embarrassment.

"Magnus, Magnus," the shouts ring from the crowd. He finally earns their respect and honor.

As Itza-Chu is walking home, he's contemplating quitting the Samra Space Program. He glances over at a hooded man in black looking at him.

"Come here, Itza-Chu," Chief Manuelito commands.

He looks very mysterious. Itza-Chu curiously stares at him. He walks toward him. His hood hides his face. The fog covers the rest of his body.

In a shrieking voice, Chief Manuelito says, "Come join us, Itza-Chu. Do you want to make this world better than what it is?"

"Of course, I do. How can I make it better?"

"We need a leader with courage and strength to fight against Maximus' World Order. We need an officer from one of his Star Ships. Do you have the skills to be a Star Ship Officer?"

"No, not yet."

"We are of the brotherhood called the Skinwalkers. We are looking for men and women who possess great skills. Would you like to join our revolution?" Chief Manuelito asks.

"Of course, I am skilled. I'm a great Novato. Nobody recognizes my talent. My younger brother always beats me in the exercises of the academy. I'm tired of that," he shouts. "Tell me more about your revolution."

"Well, we can make you better, stronger and more cunning than he. Would you like that?"

"Of course, I would," he excitedly replies.

"My name is Chief Manuelito. Come with me, my friend and I'll show you another world," he says with a smirk.

"Chief Manuelito," Itza-Chu excitedly says, "I know you as a great leader. You always helped my family. Of course, I'll join your forces to defeat this new World Order."

They shake hands. This is what Itza-Chu dreamed of someday. Taking over the planet with Chief Manuelito would galvanize him as the leader of Samra.

Suddenly, Chief Manuelito transforms into a gray large wolf.

Itza-Chu asks, "How did you do that?"

"One day, you'll know everything. You will know how to transform into the animal of your choice. Would you like that?" the wolf asks.

Itza-Chu jumps for joy. His face lights up and he says, "Yes."

The wolf whispers into his ear what he must do to become a Skinwalker. Itza-Chu smiles and hugs him. He found someone who finally believes in him.

"You know they never have respected me as a leader." His self-esteem is at its lowest and Chief Manuelito knows it.

"Itza-Chu, I'm here to take care of you. That is what I'll always do for you. I will make you the leader of the Samra Space Station."

After hours of talking about the revolution to overthrow the current World Order, Chief Manuelito says, "I need you to finish your training at the academy. Once you become an officer of one of the Star Ships, I will give you further instructions."

As they reach their destination, Chief Manuelito takes him to the mouth of a large dark cave.

"Before you enter my world, you must know—there is no

turning back, my friend. You can run back to your daddy and become one of their rats or you can run with the wolves," he sarcastically tells him.

A tremendous howling of wolves comes from deep inside the cave. Deliberately, four twenty-five-foot-high wolves walk toward Itza- Chu, their huge eyes look directly at him. There are black, brown and white wolves staring at him, which quickly transform into humans. All are Natives from the American Southwest.

The adrenalin running through his body is too much for him to handle. Itza-Chu has never seen such a powerful enlightenment of spiritual transformation between man and beast. He had read of Skinwalkers, but he believed it was a myth. Now he knows they exist. This is his dream come true.

10

SKINWALKERS

"Live your life that the fear of death can never enter your heart."
– Chief Tecumseh

Ten days later, Magnus is seen running toward a large field of trees and vegetation. He shouts, "Misty." Then a bang is heard as he transforms into Chamán. He's wearing a gold spacesuit made of Kevlar steel. A Bald Eagle adorns his red cape. His turquoise boots glow like the brown crown over his helmet at the center of which is an amethyst stone.

As he glides through the air with his arms spread on each side, he looks like a giant eagle. He's enjoying the view as he looks down at the colorful planet. It's a beautiful sunny day and everything is alive and moving.

Chamán has some of the most pleasant views of the universe and terrain from the sky, which is now a bright orange. Darkness is a delightful amethyst hue color, so it isn't ever completely dark. There are rivers and oceans of water throughout the land. People can go to the mountains or on a wilderness trip in their space car.

The trees are yellow and green. The shrubs on the mesas are bright pink and blue. Trees are as big as the Sequoias in California. Fruit and nut trees are found in abundance. The Natives call the fruit jambiya, eloton, guanabana, and chayotle. The flavor is better than humans ever savored. The nuts from the trees are red and are as big as tomatoes. They're called nuecas.

The snow isn't white, but rather rainbow-colored. From afar, it looks like cotton candy. Natural medicinal herbs brought from Earth are everywhere: sage, peppermint, alfalfa, chamomile, skullcap, cinnamon, bitter melon, ginseng, hawthorn, garlic, witch hazel, elderberry, butcher's broom, gingko biloba, valerian, turmeric, cayenne pepper, rosemary, ginger—even cannabis.

Then Chamán jets toward the elegant city of El Castillo, which has everything, including a large Spaceport. Many public space planes and rainbow-colored war spacecraft are on the ground. He has never toured the planet this way. He is full of youthful bliss. His family created a sacred kingdom in his mind. The buildings tower so high that some are above him.

He can see thousands of people of all ages and ethnicities and robots walking about enjoying the day. Loud drums are beating at a Powwow, an enormous bonfire illuminating an open pink and blue field. Chanting can be heard for miles and over a hundred male and female Natives are dancing to the beat, in feathered outfits of all colors. Deer dancers and others are prancing around, giving thanks to the Great Mother Sąmra. They have a lot to give thanks for since this planet has given them a second chance at life. The Natives from Earth believe in including all people in their traditional and cultural practices. Maximus disallows labeling people by race. Everyone is a 'human being' created by the Great Creator.

Chamán flies from building to building, marveling at the sites. There are restaurants, museums and the large Samra Aerospace Tower. There are engineers, robots and spaceships inside. It is circular and made of crystal—the most up-to-date technological space station ever built. The tower is four hundred feet high and two hundred feet in diameter—the largest building ever built in the galaxy.

Magnus clenches his right hand and points down to the south side of the city. He zooms down to a candy store. Passersby see him and he greets them with a nod. His appearance is breathtaking. They stare in disbelief. Nobody knows his identity or why he's dressed that way.

A voice from the crowd asks, "Who is that?"

Chamán sees all the candy through the outside window of the huge chocolate candy shop. There are chocolate lollipops, dark chocolate nuts and cherry-filled chocolates, his favorite. He goes inside and asks for a couple of cherry-filled dark chocolates. As he leaves the candy shop, he opens the wrapper and puts the chocolate in his mouth. The aroma of cocoa and the sweet, creamy, fruity cherry melt in his mouth. It's delicious. He lifts his right fist straight up into the air and is boosted into the stratosphere.

"Boy, that is good," he yells as he stops to look down at a forest with his x-ray vision.

He watches giraffes, lions, bears, and monkeys hanging out near a river. Yellow-green trees surround the area and pink and blue shrubs decorate the ground. It is a fascinating site to behold. His supersonic ears enable him to listen to the animal and human chatter for miles. At any given moment, Chamán can tune in on any conversation.

He's on top of a rainbow-colored mountain. Milo jumps on his head, catching him by surprise.

Milo scolds him, "Master, why are you wasting time sightseeing? We have much work to do to make sure our world is safe."

"What do you mean?"

"There's a defiant mob in the underworld who wants to destroy your father's work," Milo explains.

"Really. Who are they?" he asks abruptly.

"They are known as the 'Skinwalkers,'" Milo warns, "They are everywhere. Sometimes, you will be staring one in the face and not know it. Watch out for them because their ways are pure evil. Revenge is in their heart. Native American people have known them for a long time. They want to destroy and kill our civilization. That is why I'm here with you today."

"What do you mean?"

"I'm the only one who can recognize them, whether they are in human or animal form. They are swift, cunning and very dangerous. Only you can defeat them with your powers, Master," Milo confidently says.

Chamán appears oblivious to all that Milo has to say about Skinwalkers. Furthermore, he thinks, 'who exactly is this monkey who knows so much?' Milo knows about the history of man on Earth and Samra. This makes him feel that Milo is more than a monkey.

Chamán takes him and sits down on a rock next to the seashore. The waves are splashing against the rocks.

"Milo, teach me all you know about this world."

"Chamán, when NASA sent the first group of settlers to Samra, they were from the Apache clan. They were exiled here to create a new and better life for themselves. With the help of new space technology and satellite systems in place, the Nde people have survived. They've created a life similar to the one on Earth before the Europeans arrived. The enormous undertaking of colonizing this planet with Apache know-how and wisdom was tested on Earth. They are the only group of people who can handle such an undertaking, according to NASA scientists.

"The Apache way of life was studied for years before the Samra Space Program. Historically, they not only survived annihilation, but prospered by making the land better than what it was. Their mettle was tested in the worst parts of North America for centuries. However, even when there was no water or food, they courageously survived. New viruses like smallpox were brought by Columbus in 1492. Almost fifty million Natives were killed because of measles, influenza, chickenpox, bubonic plague, typhus, scarlet fever, pneumonia, malaria, and venereal diseases. In all, European colonizers killed around fifty-six million Native people during the first one hundred years in Southern, Central and Northern America. This caused large swaths of farmland to be abandoned. Furthermore, they had no medicinal herbs to protect them from these new diseases. All Native people on Turtle Island could have been exterminated but were not. Their use of spiritual forces to defend themselves against their enemies is a mystery to the scientific world. They use their spiritual ancestors to heal the sick. Back then, they had to travel for hours for water and food.

"Indigenous type O blood has been proven to be stronger than other blood types. Type O blood is able to adapt to any type of environment. This is why your father and mother were chosen by NASA. They took on key roles to learn and explore living on another planet. They are committed to the

Samra Space Program and have proven themselves worthy of this colossal project.

"The Apache refer to themselves as Nde, Inde, Tinde, or Tinneh, all of which mean, 'The People.' The term Apache, which is commonly used to refer to the Nde people, comes from the Zuni word Ápachu. The Ndes' passion for life has always been to protect the Earth and its inhabitants. You are people who work together because of your cultural and spiritual nature. You listen to the elders who impart their ancestors' knowledge and wisdom. It is considered a true democratic type of governance, which historically is always practiced.

"The mother is the decision-maker of the family. Her role is respected and honored by the tribe. At the age of eight, boys are separated from girls to learn different skills. The girls continue to work with and learn from their mothers and other women. They learn about the different plants and their herbal medicinal uses. Many young women go on to become herbalists and healers. Boys, on the other hand, start learning how to hunt and become warriors. They are required to identify plants. They learn the habits and characteristics of animals. They study the cycles of nature. Often, they are required to observe nature. Stalking animals for hours is part of the training. Becoming a warrior also means becoming masters of hiding and escaping.

"A story was told of Geronimo. He was a great medicine man and warrior. He was trapped inside a cave. When the American soldiers went in to find him, he was gone. He was still there, however, he had buried himself in the ground.

"The Apache Warrior is taught to have intimate knowledge of the local geography. They learn the location and names of specific trees, rocks, caves, and geographical landscapes."

"Wow, I like that my father continues the Apache tradition and culture here on Samra. Tell me more about the Skinwalkers, Milo," Chamán replies.

Milo looks around cautiously and says, "The legend of the Skinwalkers isn't well understood outside of Navajo culture. It is a hidden secret to everyone outside the tribe. Also, they do not discuss it with people they do not trust. What I'm about to tell you must not be shared with anyone. They are considered witches and they represent the antithesis of indigenous values. The community healers and cultural workers are known as medicine men and women. Witches are seen as evil. They perform harmful ceremonies and manipulative magic. It's a perversion of the good works medicine people traditionally perform. To practice their good works, traditional healers may learn about both good and evil magic. This is done to protect us against evil curses. Natives see these Skinwalkers as corrupt creatures. They have the ability to transform into animals, walking and running on all fours. Once the transformation is complete, the human witch inherits the speed, strength or cunning of the animal."

"How do you become a Skinwalker?"

"To become a Skinwalker, a Native must be initiated by an evil, secret society that requires performing the most malevolent of deeds: the killing of a close family member. After completing this task, the individual acquires supernatural powers, which enable them to shape-shift into animals. They are often seen as coyotes, wolves, foxes, cougars, dogs, and bears, but they can take the shape of any animal. Afterward, they will wear the animal skulls or antlers on their heads when they are in human form. This increases their power. They choose the animal they want to turn into, depending on the abilities needed for a particular task. Then they can return to human form in order to escape pursuers."

Chamán asks, "Are there any Skinwalkers on Samra?"

"Yes, there are. That is why we need you to be ready to defend our planet against them," Milo replies.

11

THE BOOMBOW

It concerns us to know the purposes we seek in life. Like archers
aiming at a definite mark, we shall be more
likely to attain what we want."
– Aristotle

Magnus is in his room thinking about his future. He's confused. Living a double life is taxing. How long can he hide Chamán's identity?

"Mother, I need your help," Magnus cries out.

"What is it, my child," she says as she appears before him.

"Mother, I need to know why I should be Chamán. I don't know if I can do this. I am not a man of war."

"My son, everyone has a purpose in life," Trinidad instructs. "Learn to accept who you are. Most people have been evacuated to Samra from Earth. They escaped death in their homeland. They come in the hope of building a better life. Many have jobs in mining the metal ore needed for buildings, weapons, spaceships, space planes, and robots. Others have become farmers, manufacturers and builders. Some are engineers and scientists. There are professional athletes of all sports who find happiness in entertaining the

109

community for free. Golfers have their golf courses. Galactic commerce is established. People lead wonderful lives—unlike the few who behave more like pre-technological refugees. Of course, they are taken care of by the Brotherhood Alliance. They are anti-social and isolate themselves in caves. This is where the Skinwalkers reside.

"Your father was chosen to be the Chief of the planet. Through his knowledge and wisdom, he brings hope to everyone in Samra. Of course, without the genius of Carol's advanced knowledge, this would never have happened. To many, he is their hero. Most admire him. He has made a New Order that brings peace to everyone. However, Drumpenfeurer and his assassins have caused the death of billions. He is a danger to our existence, as you know. You need to know the truth about who you are. You are the Deliverer. You will deliver order and peace to the universe. The Great Spirit has made His choice. The Prince of Darkness knows who you are. He's been trying to kill you for many years."

"Wow, Satan wants to kill me? I now understand," Magnus replies confidently while looking at his mother.

Two days later, everyone is gathered at the large coliseum for a ceremonial Powwow. Native people are dressed in their colorful feathered outfits. They are ready to pray for Samra, socialize and compete in a traditional dance competition. It is a beautiful ceremony. Native Nde-style costumes worn by all men, women and children fill the diamond-shaped marble floor, as the entrance song starts up. Drums and people chanting are heard for miles. The Great Spirit must be there listening. It's a happy event. Sacred ceremonies like this afford all an opportunity not only to give thanks through song and dance and to beat the drums, but to honor Native culture. Prayer is also a strong part of this celebration. Finally, it also brings dancers from different tribes to compete.

Dahteste feels her cheeks warm as she parades in the dance in her Native red, green and purple feathered dress. She feels proud of her culture and heritage. How she focuses on dancing to the drumbeats can be seen in her face. Trinidad is talking around a circle of fire to Native women elders.

She says, "Our drumbeats go to the universe for all to hear. Our people today represent both an end and a new beginning. Now that our enemies have broken through our strong force field, we must be more diligent and strengthen our forces. We must stop future attacks. Our weaponry, even though advanced in the universe, must be made better. Carol has invented a prototype compound bow. It will not shoot arrows like our forefathers once did. It'll shoot arrow bombs that will flare up and ignite on impact. Each arrow bomb will have the power to destroy a jet bomber a mile away."

All of a sudden, she is seen by everyone on the coliseum's jumbotron screen. She's displaying the new weapon in her hands. Everyone stops dancing and beating drums to listen. She hands the compound bow to Cochise. He loads the arrow with a silver spherical bomb on the tip and launches it into the air. It's headed toward an unmanned space car. Immediately, an array of blue and white smoke illuminates the amethyst sky. The explosion is subtle because of the atmosphere and the vessel disappears in a puff of smoke. Applause and cheers fill the air. Dahteste claps along with all the rest.

She says, "Wow. That is amazing, Momma."

Dahteste's sharp eye catches a few naysayers including elders shaking their heads. They stand still and stoic. One white-haired, light-skinned Apache woman covers her brown eyes with her wrinkled worn hands and begins to cry loudly. When she looks up, tears are running down her cheeks.

Dahteste asks, "What's wrong?"

"This weapon could have saved my son, Bobo," the woman sadly says.

"Woman, this new weapon, we hope, will save everyone's life. We call it the 'Boombow,'" Trinidad explains, as she holds it in her hand. "You can see the exquisitely detailed work of the plexiglass bow with the nylon string. Its light weight of less than two pounds is amazing. We have one thousand in production. They should be here by tomorrow."

Itza-Chu and Magnus are seen in the gathering after proudly witnessing their mother's demonstration.

"Too bad you'll never get to shoot one of them," Itza Chu says as he pushes Magnus down to the floor.

As he gets up, Golthli says, "It is time."

"Time for what, Grandpa?" Magnus asks.

"The Great Spirits are ready for you. I will see you in the small courtyard outside my home when the sun rises tomorrow," he says looking up to the sky and giving thanks with both arms raised. He walks away and vanishes into the crowd.

"Sure, Grandpa. I'll be there," Magnus replies.

He can't stop staring at his mother looking at him with her beautiful smile. He has never seen a gathering this big in his life. His eyes widen as he watches the Powwow come back to life. Throughout the coliseum, the white and black eagle feathers floating on the people's regalia look like real eagles flying around him. The sound of the drums and singing makes his skin crawl.

"Mamá, quiero aprender como usar la arma," Magnus says in Spanish. He is so eager to learn how to use the new Boombow.

"Mijo, hoy en adelante tú abuelo Golthli esta encargado de tú entrenamiento en nuestro ejército. Sin embargo, nunca digas a nadie inclusive tús hermanos. Esto es nuestro secreto. Tú eres Chamán," she excitedly reminds him.

"Mamá, voy hacer como tú?" he asks.

"Nó, tú destino es mucho más grande. Los espíritus ancianos me dijeron en un sueño que tú eres el escogido por Nuestro Creador. Necesitas aprender como navegar la nave y usar las armas, especialmente la nueva ballesta," Trinidad says.

"Mother, I always felt I was different. Even though I need a lot of preparation, I promise that I won't let you down," Magnus swears with a humble heart.

Magnus is seen waking up in the morning. His brother and sister are up already, playing chess in his room. Today is their day off from training. Dahteste is waiting for Izta-Chu to make a move. He's concentrating deeply. As she sips her orange juice through a crystal glass, Magnus sneaks out of the room.

He goes through the automated door that swooshes open and closes. He's running downhill towards Golthli's house. Kiki, his white German Shepherd robot dog, follows him wagging his tail. He's barking excitedly. Magnus is having an adrenalin rush as he scampers past boulders and trees. He enters a forest. His eye catches Milo staring at him from a green and yellow tree.

Milo says, "Listen to your heart, Master Magnus."

Caught by surprise, he glides to a stop in his Native brown clothing. He glances back at Milo who is watching him.

"What?" he asks.

"I'll tell you later," Milo mysteriously says.

"Okay, climb on board. I'll give you a lift."

Magnus continues flying through the forest with the long-roped red vines hanging from the trees. They're in his way. Milo's face looks frightened all the way to the house.

As he approaches the house, Golthli is seen in a gold dojo with a purple belt rope. He's wearing black sandals. His pink and silver bandana changes colors with the sun's reflection.

"Good morning, Grandpa," Magnus says.

"Good morning, Magnus. Did you sleep well?"

"Well, I slept like a baby."

"Very well. We have your mother's new weapon. This Boombow is a present from her. However, it must remain here. It is our secret for now, okay?"

"Yes, of course. I won't tell anyone," Magnus replies.

Cochise comes out of the hacienda house. His large, framed body is covered in a traditional Nde Indigenous vested brown shirt and Levi's. His boots are shiny black. He has two Boombows. One is strapped to his back and the other is in his hand. With his hands extended, he presents it to Magnus.

Magnus is touching the most magnificent technologically advanced weapon ever made. It makes him feel invincible. It is like having an atomic bomb in his possession. As he holds on to it, he pretends to drop it. Everyone reacts frantically.

"Got you," Magnus shouts, and they begin to laugh. "Misty," he says and quickly transforms into Chamán.

Everyone is watching with great interest at the glowing weapon now strapped to Chamán's Kevlar uniform.

"Let's go. Follow me," Golthli commands.

Walking deeper into the forest, Chamán sees the beautiful silver and pink flowers. The large green and yellow trees are twenty-five feet tall. The sandy terrain is yellow with gray rocks. They come to a huge opening on the other side of the forest. There's a turquoise river flowing down a ridge, forming a beautiful waterfall. The orange skyline is bright. Hundreds of red birds are sharing the air with spacecraft and space cars.

"Chamán, one arrow bomb can destroy a jet bomber," Cochise explains. "It can also blow up one square mile of land. Always remember that it is to be used only as a last resort. You have other powers to defeat the enemy. Use them first. If the time comes to use this weapon, it will be because you're in mortal danger. Only a few of us know how to use it."

They're facing a huge mountain called Mount SK100. There's a big black boulder over fifty feet high and weighing at least three tons.

"There's your target, my boy. Take the Boombow and load it with the arrow in your quiver. Each arrow comes with an arrowhead designed with an atomic explosive," Cochise instructs.

Chamán takes a deliberate aim at the huge bolder a mile distant. The bow is firmly grasped in his hands as he pulls the shaft from his quiver around his hip. Without taking his eyes from the target, his practiced fingers led the arrow to the rock. He raises the bow to his cheek, taking slow, deep, even breaths. He pulls the bow taut. He feels the fletching tickle to his jaw as he sights the arrow. His dominant eye aligns with the arrow. Fixing a gaze upon the target, he visualizes the desired trajectory. Even though it's a beautiful day, there's a slight gust of wind in his face. Then, with a release both swift and fluid, his fingers relinquish their grasp.

The Boombow is unleashed. It snaps forward with a resounding twang, propelling the arrow forward. The arrow soars through the air, slicing through its invisible path. They watch with anticipation as the it gracefully arcs toward its intended destination. Time seems too slow as the arrow travels. Its flight is a testament to Chamán's skill and concentration. In the culmination of the artful display, the arrow strikes its mark. It achieves a satisfying explosion and the huge brown boulder disappears in a gust of wind.

"Chamán, you have done well. Now, respect the Boombow and its precise work. One day, you will need to use all these skills to strike down Zapponata and Valdivinar," Golthli proclaims.

12

THE WENDIGO

"We, the great mass of the people, think only of our love for our land,
we do love the land where we were brought up. We will never let
our hold on this land go, to let it go will be like throwing
away our mother who gave us life."
– Native American Quote

Magnus is at his favorite secluded spot, playing with his dog Kiki and Milo, swimming in the rainbow-colored Lago Mago Lake. His laughter and his dog barking can be heard. Kiki is tempted to jump in the warm water, but he chooses not to.

The sky is lit up in a beautiful orange. After about an hour, he hears a noise behind the green and yellow trees. With his expert hearing and X-ray vision, he sees a skeletal figure fifteen feet in length and five feet in width. It has a rat face with a small nose and a gray beard. It has sunken, glowing eyes and sharp, yellow fangs. Its long arms with claws dangle down his side almost touching the ground. It has long, gray hair draping down to the waist.

Magnus has never seen such a creature. Milo stops

jumping on the rocks to notice Magnus staring at the trees. Upon closer inspection, Milo sees the Wendigo.

"Master, don't move and don't say a word," Milo warns before commanding Kiki to sit.

The creature slowly turns but looks in their direction again. After a few more minutes, it moves on.

"What was that, Milo?" Magnus asks.

"Master, it looks like a Wendigo. They have exceptional eyesight. However, if you don't move, they lose sight of you. They have acute hearing, but if you sit quietly, they won't know where you are. They have a strong sense of smell, superior strength and great speed, enabling them to stalk and overpower their victims. You can find them in cold, isolated places like caves. They can speak and whistle. That is why Native people never whistle at night. It's known that Wendigos will whistle back to get your attention. They exist only to create fear. Their spirit was once human but was turned into a Wendigo through the use of evil magic. They have an insatiable appetite for human flesh. They are fervent hunters and can attack without warning. They grow bigger the more they eat."

"Is there a cure for these creatures?"

"Not for the curse. Once someone has consumed the flesh of another, they are a Wendigo for life if they choose to join the Evil Spirit. Their spirit is forced to wander for all time. They will forever seek more flesh. Fire can get rid of them, but if you don't have access to a flame, don't move or talk. Always stand perfectly still. Be very quiet when you see one. They're too fast to outrun and too strong to outfight without fire. Wendigos do fight each other, possibly as a way to reduce competition for food. They are simply sadistic killers. Despite their frail appearance, they are immensely strong. They are capable of crushing a human skull with their bare hands. They can lift over seven-hundred-fifty pounds. They come from Turtle Island and are called other names by many Native American tribes. They are insatiable and characterized by excessive selfishness and greed. Such people evolve into human-eating monsters. They have a heart of ice."

The Wendigo circles back and hears Milo. He creeps closer to them and then dashes from the trees toward Magnus. Magnus is caught by surprise and falls with him into the lake. There is a relentless underwater wrestling match. Both are strong and sustain blows to the head and body.

Magnus yells, "Misty."

He's now Chamán. He explodes to the surface of the rainbow-colored water. In seconds, the Wendigo ascends from the water. There's blood dripping from the Wendigo's left eye. The attack resumes and there's splashing of water and grunts from the creature. The Wendigo tries relentlessly to bite through the Kevlar suit but is unsuccessful. The fight continues for hours with no end in sight. Chamán decides to fly out of the lake.

He makes it up to the orange sky and soars toward El Castillo. The Wendigo flies closely behind. Chamán passes by a window where five men are smoking cigars and playing poker.

"Wow, did you see that?" one of the poker players asks.

"No, what was it?" another asks.

"I can swear I just saw a big, gold-plated man flying in the air," he says, scratching the back of his bald head.

Next, they see both combatants on top of a roof. It's a flat surface with air conditioning vents. There are steel radar poles mounted on the roof.

The fighting resumes. Chamán is overcome with a blow

to his head. He's being choked with great force. People from the streets watch in wonder. This is the first time they have seen a Wendigo and Chamán.

Chamán breaks free and the noise of both combatants crashing against a steel post is heard by everyone. The pounding and thrashing goes on for hours. The Wendigo is frustrated and confused. Chamán reaches for his laser sword, but the creature stops him. They smash into the gray, high-rise building, breaking a few windows, and people on the streets begin dodging the falling shards of glass. However, several are struck and they lie on the ground, bleeding. Chamán looks down at the injured. Screams are loud enough to be heard everywhere.

More people are watching from their balconies. They can see him fighting the creature. Chamán momentarily loses concentration. The Wendigo puts him on his back and strikes him in the head. The animal is now twisting his helmet with both claws, trying to remove it. As it comes off Chamán's head, the monster opens its huge mouth. Its yellow fangs are salivating over its next meal.

Maximus is at home watching the battle from a large monitor in his living room. He is unable to help his son in this battle and has no access to laser blasts that could target the creature. Even if he had, it would be too risky to fire a shot without hitting Chamán. Not only is he watching the fight, but Master Juno, Melissa and Cochise are with him. They look on in horror as the Wendigo overpowers Chamán with blows to his head.

Emotions are high throughout the city. No one in the street below knows who the man in the gold steel armor is, but they start cheering for him. Chamán hears them cheering.

With a deep gasp of breath, it brings him a renewed spirit of life.

As the Wendigo prepares to take a bite of his neck, it is pulverized by Chamán's wicked forearm to its left temple. With a loud shriek, the creature flies twenty feet away and strikes its head on a steel pipe. This gives Chamán time to jump to his feet. He's armed with his laser sword. The Wendigo looks up at him, knowing full well that it only has seconds to live. It gives Chamán a sorrowful stare with his beady eyes. He rushes to the beast and swings the purple laser at it. It burns its neck. It loudly screeches and falls on its back, dead. He blasts it with two more beams and the rest of its body burns to a crisp.

Chamán is standing on the rooftop ledge looking below. He raises his right fist in the air and the people respond with uproarious applause. However, they want to know who the person in the gold suit is.

His family sits in the living room, relieved and extremely proud of this momentous victory over the dangerous Wendigo. To their knowledge, no one had ever defeated a Wendigo this way.

"Who is that man, Mom?" cries a skinny little girl, but her mother doesn't know.

Chamán flies down to the crowd. Within moments, he's over an injured child who's bleeding from his stomach. The boy, around seven-years-old, is lying on the ground and in a great deal of pain.

Chamán says, "Please give me some room to help him. What is your name young man?"

The boy looks up at him startled. "Who are you?"

"I'm known as Chamán," he proudly says as others hear his name for the first time.

The crowd begins to chant, "Chamán, Chamán, Chamán."

He looks to the stars and prays to the great spirits to heal the boy. Tata's spirit appears and joins him to heal the young man. He is no longer bleeding and the seven-inch-long gash disappears. He gets up and runs to hug his parents. They thank Chamán and joyfully walk down the street holding hands.

Hours slowly elapse and Chamán is praying over more injured. One by one, they look up and push themselves gently off the yellow ground. They thank Chamán for saving their lives. There is so much emotion that everyone wants to touch him as if he were a movie star. His passion for saving lives is enjoyable to him.

Miraculously, Trinidad shows up after everyone is gone and says, "My son, you must always remember that the Great Creator has chosen you to have these superpowers. Many will not understand what you are doing. There are countless Wendigos still roaming Samra hunting for human flesh. Keep in mind that you're here to protect our people. Even though they speak and look differently, always remember we are one tribe on this planet. We are all equal."

"What do you mean, Mother?" Chamán asks.

"These people were born in a world where the wealthy ruled through corruption and deceit. This created a divisive world, with everyone chasing after the almighty dollar. It brought on selfishness and immorality. Billions have been mercilessly killed by Zapponata and her family. However, everyone is welcome on Samra. Your father continues his well-planned evacuation program for those still trapped on Earth. With your help, we can make this planet the best in the universe. We must counteract Zapponata's stronghold on

Earth. We are developing a plan to take it back."

"Mother, nothing would make me happier than to make Earth great again," he replies with a smile.

123

13

EVACUATION

"Be strong, but not rude. Be kind, but not weak. Be humble, but not timid. Be proud, but not arrogant."
– Native American Proverb

Ten years later, Valdivinar controls the Earth. His mother and Satan support his evil rule. He sits on his throne in Solorio. He can see crowds of people from all over the world celebrating his dictatorship on the large wall monitor.

The crowd repeatedly yells, "Valdivinar the Great One. No one is greater than he."

He portrays himself as a benevolent, loving ruler. He can only be around people who tell him how wonderful he is. He is unable to handle any criticism, which makes it difficult for people to survive if they disagree with him. However, those people loyal to him and his regime are well taken care of. Those who disagree with him live on rationed food and water. Many are homeless and in hiding.

Valdivinar is dreaming of the missile explosions killing men, women and children around the world. Those who live in the suburbs and survive pillage the streets. Many run into stores and come out with armfuls of groceries. There is no order and no police to stop them. His government is established to encourage the 'survival of the fittest.'

Many fights and shootings take place every day. Everyone carries a laser blaster, including children. If famine, pestilence, air pollution, or bombs don't kill them, then they kill each other. The world population is facing extinction at the hands of Valdivinar.

Charities like the Red Cross run food banks. Chaos is ubiquitous as lines of people can be seen for miles in every country, begging for food and water. They provide bread, soup and hot beverages to those who can't afford them. Valdivinar doesn't believe that it is his duty to aid people. That leaves private citizens, organizations and charities to develop world soup kitchens to help others. One of these organizations is a secret society called The Rainbow Alliance. This small group is an underground organization set up by Matthew in Silver City, New Mexico. Their mission is to provide those in need with food, water, shelter, weapons, and clothing. The ultimate goal is to evacuate them to Planet Samra. This program is in its fifteenth year. It brings hope to those who want a better opportunity for a life of freedom. Matthew oversees this worldwide organization. The aftermath of the Battle of Tears didn't disseminate the NASA Command Center in the house. This is unknown to Valdivinar. Matthew orchestrates evacuations from here with his son.

"Maximus, how is everyone?" he asks.

"Dad, I'm happy to report that your grandchildren are

doing great. All three are now officers of the Samra Space Program. They have their own Star Ship and fly on daily missions, protecting us from enemy invasions. How is everything on Earth?"

"I'm sad to report that we lost around twenty thousand this month on Turtle Island. I don't have a count of our dead from other countries. The food and clothing you bring to us every month are given to people around the world and they are grateful. Thank you, son." Matthew replies.

"It's an honor to help. Our Great Spirit speaks to my soul every day. We will continue to rescue people. I don't know how much longer they can survive. Valdivinar's lust for blood is never-ending."

"Son, we have two hundred thousand more immigrants in Mexico City ready to be evacuated. When will your ships be ready?" he urgently asks. But the radio transmission is lost. Matthew clicks his radio but gets no response from Maximus.

"Son, are you there? Over. This is Dr. Hogan calling, over. Are you there?"

Matthew changes frequencies on his radio. He believes La Azteca is on the move somewhere in the stratosphere. There are layers of Earth's atmosphere that lie between the troposphere and the mesosphere. The lower part of the stratosphere is nearly isothermal (a layer of constant temperature), whereas temperatures in its upper levels increase with altitude. It contains the ozone layer, which shields the Earth from the sun's ultraviolet radiation. This may cause a loss of radio transmission. However, Maximus' ship is struck by several meteors on the starboard side. The vessel is hit so hard that the impact causes damage to its communications network.

Maximus is by his microphone, sitting in front of his large

window, inside the unlit Command Center. A loud siren is heard throughout the ship. He can see only a panoramic view of Planet Earth.

"Johnny Bear, we lost power in the Command Center. How much power can you give me?" he asks.

"Chief, I'm doing the best I can. I'm powering another generator. I'll get you power in ten minutes. However, we were hit hard down here. We're cleaning up the mess at the same time, sir."

Johnny Bear is wearing a blue space suit. He's a short Apache and is the Chief Engineer. He scampers around to the control panel in the engineering room, the heart of the vessel, and he is in control of its every movement. There are large, ten by ten foot silos filled with energy derived from the ten thousand kilowatt generator. He touches it and burns himself. His assistant comes to his aid as he lifts him from the floor. His head is bleeding but he's conscious.

"Johnny Bear, what's going on?" Maximus says in frustration from the darkened Command Center. "I need power. We're not moving."

"I'll get some power to you soon, Chief," he quickly replies.

Maximus is looking at a huge asteroid headed toward the ship from his window.

"Impact of asteroid in ten seconds," Carol's voice is heard on the intercom.

Maximus asks, "Johnny Bear, where's that power?"

"It's coming, sir. Give me a few more minutes," he says.

"Push it with all you got. We're sitting ducks," Maximus says anxiously.

"I'm just about done. Hold on. Got it. Here you go."

Johnny Bear grabs a hammer and bangs the pump valve

next to him twice, unclogging the pipes. The craft moves forward and outside communication is restored.

"Son, are you there, over?" Matthew asks.

Maximus is exhausted but relieved.

"Yes, Father, I'm here. Everything is taken care of and we're headed your way. We should be there in around ten minutes. Where will this evacuation take place?"

Matthew sits in his chair and says, "They'll be waiting for your vessels in Mexico City. I'm sending you the GPS coordinates right now. I'm so proud of you. You can't imagine how much inspiration you are to all of us. You are their only hope of survival. I read President Thomas Jefferson once said, 'Evil triumphs when good men do nothing.' Keep up the good work."

"Father, you taught me to be who I am. Don't forget that," Maximus replies over the radio.

The NASA Spaceships land in Mexico City. As the spacecraft doors open, from below, a bright light illuminates the ground. The evacuees are standing in astonishment.

Carol's voice comes on the intercom, "Bienvenidos amigos. Favor de embarcarse por las puertas abiertas. Muchas gracias."

Everyone slowly climbs up the ramp to the open entrance of each ship. The enormous vessels are at capacity with hungry yet happy immigrants from this region. Maximus watches by his monitor as every evacuee is given food and water as they enter their respective spaceship. Families cry in disbelief. They have never seen spaceships this large.

Once everyone is onboard, Carol says, "Maximus,

everyone is aboard and accounted for. We're ready to close the doors and begin the launch countdown."

Maximus orders all his Spaceship Officers over the radio, "Attention everyone, we'll leave in ten seconds. Get ready for blastoff."

Just then, Carol comes on the speaker, "An enemy ship is in the area. We must leave now."

Maximus is sitting in the cabin seat and looks out the window. He sees La Mata Raza in the distance.

"Are the engines ready to go?" he asks Johnny Bear.

"We're ready to go, Chief."

"Go," Maximus commands.

All ships are up in the air. With a quick blast of speed, they leave the Earth's stratosphere.

Drumpenfeurer, from La Mata Raza's Command Post says, "Fire, fire."

There are huge red canon shots fired at Maximus' fleet. They maneuver to avoid being struck. However, one of the ships is hit.

"Maximus, we have been hit. I can't control the ship. We're going down," Samra Space Officer Lujan says.

The spacecraft with everyone onboard explodes. In disbelief, Maximus looks at the horrific explosion from his monitor in the Command Station. He knows the young officer and his family from Silver City. It is never easy for him to see people die during these evacuations. But it is a risk everyone takes. The sad truth is that La Mata Raza reminds him of the Border Patrol helicopters when he was a kid.

14

THE WATCHMEN

*"We warned that one day you would not be able to control what you
have created…That day is here."*
– Chief Arvol Looking Horse

Magnus, now thirty-one years old, is cruising above Samra in Thumbelina. The day is gorgeous. The bright orange sky illuminates the city.

He looks out his window from the Command Post, boasting long, jet-black hair. He now stands six feet two inches. His slim muscular body fits nicely in the ivory-white officer's uniform. He enjoys wearing the high-collar shirt with crystal stones. A brown, white and yellow Bald Eagle is embroidered on the back. His brown and turquoise stone crown adorns his head, a gift from his grandmother.

Magnus enjoys Powwow music. Native drumbeats and chanting play over the ship's speaker. He's sitting in his glass seat with a matching table in front of a gold computer. He stares out the huge window, as he flies over El Castillo. His staff of engineers and Novatos are on a patrol mission with him. They're dressed in blue uniforms with the same high-collared top and Bald Eagle logo.

There's a lot of activity in the control room monitoring the atmosphere. Magnus views El Castillo through a monitor. The weather brought a lot of energy and increased activity to the city. People fly their space cars. Kids race on their flying skateboards. Ten teenagers are air soaring. They look like giant eagles in their gold bird-caped suits. The flowers bring out every beautiful color imaginable. It is a remarkable sight. He feels like he's living his dream.

He notices a mass of people on the monitor, cheering on their racehorses at the Maximus Racetrack. People come to be entertained by these athletic thoroughbreds. His father wants horse racing on the planet. He was brought up at the Del Mar Racetrack in California, where his parents took him every weekend. The biggest difference is that gambling isn't allowed. It is considered a form of temptation to have wealth and is not a Native American belief. The winning horse's trainer, therefore, is given a trophy. Those people who bet on the winner are given coupons, which they can redeem for extra food or clothing.

Ten miles from the racetrack, Magnus visits Samra Stadium. This stadium is built for both indoor and outdoor sports. He can see a baseball game going on. The score is five to four. Samra Dodgers are winning in the bottom of the seventh inning against the Samra Padres.

Many baseball players were rescued by Maximus and successfully evacuated from Earth. They brought their expertise and equipment with them and volunteered to play for the people of Samra for free. They are grateful to be alive and still be playing in front of fans. This brought so much happiness to everyone. It showed a spirit of playing for the fun of the game. These athletes truly want to have fun again without having to contend with the massive egos of the team owners.

He hears the crack of the bat and the ball goes flying into the crowd. As the Padre player runs around the bases, the crowd stands up and gives him a great ovation. Baseball is played all year. There is a final championship game played by the two best teams. This is exactly like a World Series, except it is called The Series of the Universe. In football, the Superbowl name stays the same.

"My son," Trinidad says, suddenly appearing before him and Milo.

"Mother, it's good to see you again," Magnus says.

Her body appears almost like a ghost. She's wearing a black gown with a black veil. Milo appears startled. This is the first time he has seen Trinidad's spirit.

"Milo, I didn't mean to scare you," she says smiling.

Milo stares at her, dumbfounded by her presence.

"Carol, your grandmother and I are preparing a plan to invade Valdivinar's Empire on Earth," she says.

"Hello, Magnus. How are you?" Carol asks.

"Hello, my grandson," Melissa chimes in on his monitor.

Milo is overwhelmed by all of them coming at him at once.

"We've uncovered a weakness in Valdivinar's military. We might have an ally who can help us on Earth," Carol explains. "Chamán needs to fly to a place in Mexico called El Gigante. Historically, it is truly a gigantic area with several ancient pyramids that are painted red. No one knows when they were built or who built them. We need to know if the structures are still there. Under them are subterranean humanoids. I've been monitoring them. Their purpose is to make Earth's natural resources like oil and metals. With their help, we feel confident that we can take back our planet. Perhaps restore it to life."

"This is a highly sacred place for the Spirit World," Trinidad adds. "This area is unknown to Valdivinar. Chamán needs to contact the underground humanoids."

"Grandson," Melissa chimes in, "We need to contact the underworld that we believe exists there."

"So, there's life in this ancient place," Magnus comments.

"This place is still sacred to the people who live there," Carol explains. "Not everyone believes in such a legend. In the Bible, Enoch tells us that our Creator appointed two hundred angels under the leadership of a trusted Archangel. They watched over the humans that were cast out from Eden. Over time, 'Watchmen' began to covet human life. They married and had children. The Watchmen's leader bound them with an oath to rebel against our Great Creator. Their offspring were hybrids of angels and humans and grew to enormous heights. The Greek Titanoi and the Norse Jotten all bear similarities to the Nephilim in the Book of Enoch. The Watchmen were imprisoned in an abyss on Earth, a spiritual realm under the Earth's surface where they await their final judgment. They are forbidden to enter Heaven and be embraced by the love of our Creator. For this reason, some have chosen to rebel and harm the humans sent to them. They have become demons and torment humans to this day. It is believed that evil originated from these corrupted angels. They are also known as copper serpents, brazen hydras and water serpents. They resemble the praying mantis. We believe they came before the creation of man on Earth. They have great significance in the world."

"What do you want me to find out?" Magnus asks.

"We want to make them our friends," Carol replies.

"Chamán is to go underground and find their leader. There is a subterranean ocean that has human-like movement. He must explore this area and make contact with them. They are highly sophisticated and technologically advanced humanoids."

"Some are good and some are cruel," Trinidad warns. "The reason for their cruelty is that they are envious of us who are able to live above ground. Also, they aren't worthy of love from our Creator. However, they can help us defeat Valdivinar if they choose to do so. Please find a way to get them on our side. Right now, they are concerned about how long the Earth can last under his rule. We have been told that Valdivinar is pumping too much oil and taking too many minerals from the Earth. These natural resources which Our Mother has given us are running out."

"I understand. I'll prepare my crew and leave as soon as possible. Carol, please send me the GPS coordinates for El Gigante, Mexico," Magnus responds.

"For this mission," Carold answers, "Cochise and Golthli will join you."

"Agreed," Magnus responds, smiling.

One day later, Magnus is sitting in his swivel chair onboard Thumbelina. They are about to depart for El Gigante. There are five thousand Novatos onboard, all dressed in blue Kevlar spacesuits.

"Johnny Bear," Magnus says on the intercom, "do we have enough copperlyum to reach Earth?"

"Yes, sir. We have enough of that hyper matter for faster-than-light travel for up to 30 days," Johnny Bear answers from the engineering room.

There are several huge silver silos filled with copperlyum fuel in the engineering room. Copperlyum is found in the mines near the City of Zoey. It energizes all spacecraft into hyperspace. It's also traded to other space centers in the universe.

"Power us up, Johnny," Magnus commands. "We need to reach Earth as quickly as possible. Energize in five, four, three, two, one."

The spaceship reaches top speed in seconds. Magnus is seated, looking out the bridge's large window with Golthli and Cochise. Occasionally, asteroids or meteorites fly past them. The vessel is huge. However, it could still be destroyed by the impact of an asteroid the size of a small apartment. The ship has excellent radar and sonar equipment for protection. Both instruments can detect enemy spaceships, as well. So far everything is going smoothly. Everyone onboard thinks this is a rescue mission as they had been told. However, this is a secret mission for Chamán. Dr. Matthew Hogan was contacted by Carol earlier in the week regarding this secret mission to meet the Watchmen.

Ten days later, Chamán is standing at the mouth of a dark, foggy cave. It's a windy and rainy day in El Gigante, Mexico. Even though it is daytime, the cave is dark and ice-cold.

Golthli is standing next to Chamán and says, "Be strong. Use all of your powers, including reading their minds. Share with them your wisdom and knowledge. Make them feel you come as a friend. Remember, they control all of the oil and natural resources. They allow these resources to be drilled and mined. Their genetics aren't that much different than ours. Good luck!"

Cochise, standing next to him adds, "We will be listening and watching everything. You might hear weeping and gnashing of teeth by those trapped in the abyss. All are waiting for judgment day, according to the Creator. Be careful, my brother."

All three hug.

"Okay, here I go," Chamán says as his eyes turn to bright white lights.

He begins his descent through the first layer of rocks blocking the cave. He's at a depth of 1000 meters. It is cold but he's able to regulate his body temperature. The light from his eyes illuminates the cave. He can see at least twenty feet ahead as he breaks through the Earth's crust. Moments later, he can see flying giant condors, ants, praying mantises, and bats. He hears the weeping and gnashing of teeth growing louder. He senses someone is watching him. He stops and waits. The ambiance in the cave is ominous. The walls are light orange and brown. The ground is sandy and white. It smells like horse manure. Beyond the wall, he can see humans crying in misery, though they appear almost lifeless. With their eyes wide open, they are calling out for mercy and forgiveness. There is what appears to be a male giant guarding them. Then he sees twenty-five red giant creatures moving slowly in his direction. They have two large gray wings on their backs, two long arms, and large claws. Their legs are hairy and bony. Each has two horns on its forehead. Frightening and freaky, they have fiery blue eyes that radiate throughout the cave. Suddenly, behind them appears an even larger orange creature, presumably the leader.

The orange creature asks in a deep loud voice, "Who are you?"

"My name is Chamán, and I was born on this planet years ago. Now I am living on a distant planet. "With whom am I speaking?" Chamán asks politely.

"You may call me the Watcher. Why are you here?"

"I come in peace to save the Earth from destruction," Chamán answers.

"How do you plan on saving this planet?" he asks while moving around the cave, laughing. Others join in, their laughter echoing inside the chamber.

Chamán replies in his deep voice, "I come from the family of the Apache tribe that lived here for thousands of years."

"We know the Apache people. You are highly respected by us," the Watchman says as he approaches Chamán, sniffing his clothes. Chamán tries to remain calm.

"We have always listened to our Creator and took good care of the Earth when we were here," Chamán explains. "Also, we only took from the land what was needed to survive. Drilling and fracking for oil is against our nature. Mining for gold, silver, copper, ore, and coal was the white man's choice. This came from men of greed. We fought for Mother Earth. However, their forces were too powerful for us to stop them."

"Chamán, I know you left us. Now we see much more oil and minerals being taken. This is to satisfy Valdivinar's lust for power. What do you propose?" the Watcher asks.

"We wish to take back this planet… with your help," Chamán proposes. "Can you stop Valdivinar from getting these natural resources? If so, he would lose his military power, unable to make weapons and missiles. Then we can attack him soon."

"You ask too much from me, my young friend. Our Creator has given us the duty to protect the Earth. For thousands of years, we have done so. Now you come to put a stop to our way of life? Who are you?" he proclaims loudly.

"What can I do to show you we can defeat Valdivinar? He shows no remorse for killing people and has no regard for the planet."

"You must prove to me that you are the chosen one. For centuries, we were told that a person with great powers would come to us to save Mother Earth. Through this powerful person, we could change the world. How do I know you are this person?" the Watchman asks, stepping away.

"First, I want to thank you for showing kindness to the poor innocent people suffering from hunger and lack of shelter. We know what you are doing to help them. My father, Maximus, has provided a safer place for them on a planet called Samra. He has the military wherewithal to defeat Valdivinar's army. When this is done, we will bring peace and harmony back to this land. I promise that we will take better care of the land, water, plants, animals, and humans. We didn't do it for centuries, but I pledge that we will if you give us another chance," Chamán says.

"I like your words, and I see that you're an honest young man. However, you aren't the leader, are you?" he asks.

"No, I am not. My father is the leader of our people," he answers.

"Okay, then I need one thing from you before I make my decision," the Watcher replies. "Yes, anything," Chamán answers.

"Bring me the body of Valdivinar's son as proof that you are the Chosen One," the Watcher says as he retreats into the darkness.

15

MISSION IMPOSSIBLE

"Do not grieve. Misfortunes will happen to the wisest and best of men. Death comes always out of season. It is the command of the Great Spirit. And all nations and people must obey."
– Big Elk, Omaha

Upon returning home to El Castillo, Magnus meets privately with his parents, Cochise, Melissa, Matthew, Golthli, and Carol at the Samra Space Station Command Center. Inside a large office, they sit around a glass-framed table with steel chairs in Maximus' office. They are anxious to hear Magnus speak about his journey to the center of the Earth to meet the underground humanoids. Magnus smiles at everyone as they all wait nervously for him to speak.

"Good morning, everyone," Magnus begins. "As you've heard, the Watcher wants proof that Chamán is the Chosen One. That proof comes with a price. He wants me to deliver Drumpenfeurer to them."

Carol comes on the speaker, "Good morning, everyone. Based on our satellite spyware of Earth, we can send our

Mother Ships with our jet battleships to Earth. They will need one thousand Boombows. Each Eagle 7000 will have twenty-five Boombows mounted inside the battleship, ready to fire. We have the technology to open the Boombow hatch and shoot the arrow bombs at the enemy's vessels. The canon laser blasters should be highly effective in the initial attack on the enemy's fast jet bombers."

"I agree, Carol," Maximus says. "We'll need all our military strength on our planet to make this work. It'll be an all-out attack. I'll contact all our bases to prepare for battle. Chamán will lead the battle from Thumbelina. La Azteca will pick up more evacuees in Japan during the attack. Are there any questions?"

"Father, I want Itza-Chu and Dahteste with me on Thumbelina. I'm going to use them and their special Star Ships to attack Drumpenfeurer. I'll strategically place them close to Drumpenfeurer's monster vessel. They will work together to draw him out. We need to take him alive. Chamán will sort things out to bring him on board Thumbelina," Magnus says.

Suddenly, Trinidad's voice is heard, "Please watch over them, my son. I sense there is still resentment in Itza-Chu's heart about your position as a Commander. Be careful how you use him in battle."

"Mother, you know my brother. He's a brave and skillful officer. He's shown unwavering loyalty to the Samra Space Program and has fought in many battles against foreign enemies from other planets. Remember the time he saved the planet? He fought so bravely against the evil Sintipholops from the planet Zanglofort. His vessel shot down twenty of their spacecrafts. How about when the Zengoldorps invaded us last year? He sounded the alarm that prompted everyone to prepare for battle. He led the attack that made us victorious."

"My son, always remember to watch your back," Trinidad says calmly, "even if it means not trusting your own family."

"Something is troubling me about this mission," Magnus replies.

"What's that?" Carol asks. "We have the military and the weaponry to get to Zapponata."

"Is there a chance for us to take over Earth? I miss it so much," Magnus proclaims.

Everyone looks at him sadly. They understand he's always wanted to go back to make it a better place.

Maximus says, "Son, we pray that the day will come to return to Earth. It is not for selfish reasons, but because we are its protectors. We are given the innate talent to nurture Mother Earth. It's God-given. This will never leave us, no matter where we are. We are taking care of Samra and she is happy. You can see the beautiful life we have for everyone. There is love and peace amongst our people. We want that to continue. As for returning to Earth or staying here, you will decide when the time comes. Know one thing, my son: What you decide will be your choice and no one else's."

"Thank you, father," he happily answers.

At that moment, everyone slowly disperses from the room. Milo jumps on Magnus' shoulder as he exits through a sliding glass door. Milo begins to scratch his head.

"So, what are we doing today, Master?" he asks.

"Oh, not much. I need to prepare to attack Drumpenfeurer," Magnus says with confidence as they walk toward the City of El Castillo.

"Is that all?" Milo jokes.

"Milo, we're going to be in the biggest battle we've ever

fought. All our warriors must be ready for war against him."

"Master, indeed, this battle is going to prove who is the dominant force of the universe."

"The Dodgers are playing the Giants tonight at the stadium," Magnus says. "Let's go watch the game."

"Let's go. You know I'm always ready to see the Dodgers beat the Giants."

Magnus and Milo jump off a space car and walk inside the baseball stadium. They hear the roar of the crowd, cheering a homerun from a Dodger. They found their front-row seats behind the Dodgers' dugout. It is a packed house. They watch all nine innings. The Dodgers win the game 10-4. Everyone leaves the game very happy.

Five days later, Maximus is standing with Master Juno inside the huge coliseum. Novatos, warriors and officers are standing in line listening—all ten thousand combatants who will be headed toward Earth shortly.

"Welcome, everyone," Maximus begins. "As you know, we're sending you in harm's way. It will be a long dog fight in space. We have the best spacecraft and weapons for your use, but it'll take your best skills and experience to defeat the enemy's defenses. Our Great Creator will be with you and we will too. Commander Magnus will be in charge of the attack on board Thumbelina."

"Everyone ready?" Master Juno shouts.

Everyone answers, "Yes, sir."

"Go to your assigned Mother Ship and prepare to launch."

"Yes, sir," everyone shouts as they excitedly run to board their ships.

The newly designed eagle-shaped Mother Ships are covered in rainbow-colored, triple-coated epoxy paint for extra protection from enemy fire. They look magnificent.

Dahteste walks up to Magnus in his Command Post with Itza-Chu. She is now almost forty years old. Her long black hair is hanging down to her waist. She has beautiful green eyes. Her suit is all blue with a brown and white Bald Eagle logo.

Everyone on board Thumbelina listens as Carol announces, "T minus ten seconds and counting. Everyone get ready to launch."

As the countdown gets to 'one,' the rainbow-colored metal birds lift off their platforms—a beautiful sight to behold. The bright orange sky is filled with colorful vessels zooming through the atmosphere without a hitch. In ten days, they'll be in Earth's stratosphere ready for battle.

"Come in, Drumpenfeurer, over," Chief Manuelito says from inside his cave. He's using a radio that Itza-Chu stole from the Samra Space Station.

"Yes, amigo. How can I help you today?" Drumpenfeurer asks, laughing, as he sits drinking at a Russian bar.

"Maximus' fleet just launched and they're headed toward Earth. They should arrive in your orbit in ten days. They're sending a fleet of ten Mother Ships with one hundred Eagle 7000 Dog Fighters. Each one will carry twenty-five Boombows and two canon laser blasters," Chief Manuelito reports.

"What the heck are you talking about? How did they come up with all that artillery? There's no way they can beat us. Is Itza-Chu still on our side?"

"Yes, he is. He's not going to hurt you. He's ready for orders."

"Good. We'll need his help to get out of this battle. I'll let everyone know. We'll be ready. Over and out," Drumpenfeurer says as he lowers his wrist phone to his side in disbelief.

He pauses for a moment, confused.

"Dad, are you there?"

"Yes, son. What's up?" Valdivinar says as he sits on his bed in Solorio.

"Chief Manuelito just called to warn us that Maximus' army is headed our way. They should be here in ten days."

Valdivinar laughs and says, "Seriously?" He shakes his head in disbelief.

He's wearing purple-colored pajamas and watching a Batman movie with his wife. He takes out a cigarette from a golden case and lights it as he paces in the dark room.

"Most of my life, my parents never trusted me. I had to figure out how to win them over. They made no sense, nor did they have the know-how to plan attacks and train an army. What am I going to do? This is the first time someone is attacking us with that much force."

Valdivinar's pajamas are wet with perspiration. His forehead drips with sweat as he listens to Drumpenfeurer's description of Maximus' large army weapons. He is afraid of the Boombow. He can't rely on his silver tongue to stop this attack.

With his knees shaking and lips trembling, he tells his son, "This is the first time in my life that I feel afraid."

He tries to wipe sweat from his face with his pajama sleeve. However, it's wet.

"How do I make all of this go away?" he asks his son.

"Don't let Grandma hear you say that, all right? She'll think you're weak and disloyal. As your son, I know that you're merely a narcissist."

"Guilty as charged, my son."

Valdivinar walks out to his balcony overlooking the city. He drops the cigarette and puts it out with his black slipper.

Ten days later, the invasion begins. Magnus is at the Command Post in Thumbelina with Milo, Cochise and Golthli. It's eagle-shaped and clearly the largest space vessel hovering over Earth. The sun is shining and the spaceship's rainbow paint is glowing.

"Attention, everyone. We'll be arriving at our target in twenty seconds," Carol announces.

Then an explosion is heard in the distance. One of their Mother Ships is destroyed in a puff of white smoke. Red Drumpenfeurer missiles are fired from every direction.

Then, Magnus' ship is struck on the starboard side and he announces on the radio, "This is an ambush. They know we're here. "Novatos, get to your Eagle 7000 Dog Fighters. Fast."

Carol shouts, "Emergency. Thumbelina's engine room is severely hit. The outer panel is fried. Small transformers and contactors need to be replaced. The space dock door is jammed and none of our Eagle 7000 Dog Fighters can get out."

"What's going on?" shouts Dahteste as she is in her

cockpit ready for the dog fight.

"Dahteste, don't worry. They need to fix the payload door. Everyone must wait until we are all ready to attack, just as we planned," Carol replies.

"Yes, let's wait," Izta-Chu agrees from the cockpit of his Super Star Ship. It's black and larger than the Eagle 7000 Dog Fighters.

Two droids are seen on the outer platform, unscrewing a panel from Thumbelina. They are two feet high and look like yellow eggs with two round rubber wheels. Metallic noise can be heard from the interior as they go about their work, replacing the transformers and contactors. The doors suddenly open and the vessels are off awaiting orders. Taking the lead is Chamán in his star ship.

"Attention officers, I am Chamán. I can now reveal our mission. It is to destroy La Mata Raza and take Drumpenfeurer prisoner. If he resists, you have the green light to do whatever it takes to bring him to me alive."

This is the first time Chamán has taken over a Star Ship battle. Itza-Chu is enraged and confused. He is there to protect Drumpenfeurer and his assassins. He didn't expect to be in the middle of something this big with Chamán.

Fighting begins in all directions. Dahteste is fearlessly knocking out several B4000 assassin jet bombers. Her precise maneuvers are noticed by Drumpenfeurer from La Mata Raza. Her craft is moving up and down and side to side, blasting enemy vessels with great skill.

Drumpenfeurer is engaged in the battle. He and Itza-Chu make eye contact as they come face to face from inside their cockpits. Itza-Chu gives him the thumbs up and flies away.

Dahteste says on the radio, "I have Drumpenfeurer in my sights."

Itza-Chu hears her and then turns his ship around to get a visual. He is sweating, wondering what to do.

Drumpenfeurer is a sitting duck. With all the loud canon laser blasts going on in the air, no one else is in the area. Dahteste and Drumpenfeurer now face off. She fires first, squarely hitting his cockpit. He's dazed and sweating in his orange space suit, blood dripping from his forehead. He's still conscious, though his ship is twirling out of control. He regains control of his vessel and aims at Dahteste's Star Ship. Itza-Chu is drenched in sweat as he watches Drumpenfeurer, who is ready to fire at Dahteste without her knowledge.

Dahteste says on the radio, "I just shot Drumpenfeurer's ship. Chamán, you can come and capture him."

Itza-Chu says, "No, I can't do this. I can't kill Dahteste."

He closes his eyes. Suddenly, he hears a huge blast. He opens his eyes and Dahteste's Star Ship is destroyed by Drumpenfeurer's red laser blast. Itza-Chu is crying out of control.

"No," a scream from Trinidad is heard as she appears in the sky.

Chamán can only see that Dahteste's Star Ship has exploded. He's about to blast La Mata Raza with a Boombow from his ship. With the press of the blue button inside his vessel, the evilest spaceship ever built explodes with a huge bang. It is vaporized. Now, he's looking for Drumpenfeurer.

Carol tells everyone on the radio, "Dahteste's Star Ship has been shot down."

"La Mata Raza is no more. I've shot her down," Chamán says in a loud voice.

He flies swiftly to where Dahteste was last seen. He spots Drumpenfeurer's damaged craft and fires a blue laser blast shot at it. It starts spinning out of control.

Chamán opens his cockpit window and flies toward his enemy's spacecraft. He swoops it from the air and hoists it on his back. He's flying toward Thumbelina with Drumpenfeurer and his spacecraft. In minutes, he reaches the ship's payload entrance. He places the vessel on the launch pad then carries an unconscious Drumpenfeurer to a secluded room. He leaves him there and walks to his Command Post to make an announcement.

Grabbing the radio, he says, "Officers, you can go to your Mother Ships. This part of the mission is complete. We have Drumpenfeurer in custody. Thank you for your bravery."

Chamán can see the remaining Eagle 7000 Dog Fighters flying back to their Mother Ships from Thumbelina's window.

16

A GREAT SORROW IN MY HEART

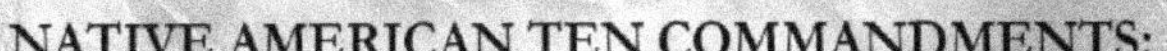

Melissa is on the radio from Samra's Command Space Center, calling her husband as tears run down her cheeks.

"My love, come in, over."

"My love, hearing you're alive and well soothes my heart. How is everyone? Did we get Drumpenfeurer?"

"Yes, we have him in custody," she says. "He's crying like a baby. He wants his mama. So much for being a brave man. We're going to deliver him to the Watchmen today. I have some bad news. Our grandchild was shot down during the battle."

"Poor Itza-Chu," he sadly replies on the radio.

"No, no, it isn't Itza-Chu. Dahteste is gone," she says, crying.

"What? Oh, my God. No. My little grandchild is gone?" he replies, crying.

"Yes, she's gone with the Great Spirit. She died with honor," Melissa sadly replies.

"She's with our great ancestors in the spirit world," he agrees.

Matthew, sitting in NASA's Space Command Center in Silver City, wipes away tears.

"Dr. Hogan, this is Carol," he hears her voice on his radio, "My condolences for your loss. She was a brave and intelligent Apache Warrior. I'll never forget her positive attitude."

"Thank you, Carol," he sadly replies.

"We need you to send an update to the Watchmen," Carol commands. "Tell them Chamán will deliver Drumpenfeurer to them tomorrow morning at the cave entrance in El Gigante."

He pauses to collect himself then says, "I'll send the message right now."

There is much sorrow and confusion with the news that Dahteste has died. Meanwhile, Drumpenfeurer is in custody, screaming for mercy and demanding to be let go.

He hollers, "You can't hold me here as a political prisoner. That's against the Constitution."

Chamán scoffs at him. "So, you think we're going to let you go because you're from a powerful family? You think you're immune from prosecution?"

"Who are you?" Drumpenfeurer demands.

"My name is Chamán," he says in his deep, mysterious voice. It made his enemy shake with fear.

His face is soaked in sweat as he kneels in a ten-by-ten-foot room. His surroundings are completely gray with little but a bed and a red blanket. It's thirty degrees Celsius inside the room.

"You can't keep me here. My father is the most powerful man on Earth," he yells.

"I know who your father is. He will soon meet his demise as foretold by our ancestors," Chamán promises him. "Who killed my sister Dahteste?"

"Your sister? I'm sorry…I don't remember," Drumpenfeurer answers sarcastically.

Chamán uses his superpower to read his mind. "He is the one," he says to himself. "He killed my sister."

He wants to kill Drumpenfeurer on the spot, but he didn't want to break his promise.

The next day, Chamán brings Drumpenfeurer to the

mouth of the El Gigante cave. Both are standing in front of it at dawn. They are surrounded by a heavy mist. Suddenly, a loud growling sound can be heard inside the cave. Drumpenfeurer is unaware of what is going on and is trembling with fear. Then, out of the cave come five red creatures. One is the orange-colored Watchman. Their large bodies with black horns and gray wings scare him so much that he urinates on himself.

The Watcher says in a deep metallic voice, "You have done well, Chosen One. In my book, you have great courage. I am very impressed with you."

"I have fulfilled my part of the agreement. Now, you must fulfill yours," Chamán insists.

"A promise is a promise. We will allow no more oil or minerals to be placed into the hands of your enemy," the Watcher swears.

"What are you talking about?" Drumpenfeurer shouts. "You can't stop my father. He's a god. Nobody on Earth can stop him. He'll kill every one of you. You don't know how powerful he is."

"Silence," the Watcher says as a bright red beam of lightning comes from his eyes and strikes Drumpenfeurer's right leg.

Blood starts dripping from where it hit him. The Watcher looks at the blood but knows he must restrain himself from attacking his prey.

"He's in your hands now. I must go back to Samra. I want to thank you for taking care of the Earth and our good people. I hope one day we can live in peace with you, in this sacred land," Chamán says as he walks back to Thumbelina.

As he enters his ship, he can hear Drumpenfeurer yelling at the top of his lungs, begging for mercy.

He screams, "Chamán, save me."

Thumbelina shoots across the sky and heads home.

The Watcher grabs Drumpenfeurer by his long, yellow hair and drags him into the dark cave. He is gone forever.

Ten days later, in Itza-Chu's messy bedroom, Maximus is talking to his son about Dahteste's death.

"My son, please tell me what you saw when your sister was shot down," he sadly says.

Itza-Chu is dressed in a casual black hoodie and black workout nylon pants. He's on his way to a football game with his Skinwalker friends. However, now he feels trapped by his father.

He's tense and scared to the point that Maximus asks him, "Are you okay?"

"Father, I didn't see anything. I was fighting just like everyone else," he replies while sitting on the edge of his bed with his head down.

Suddenly, Trinidad appears in the room. "Itza-Chu, what have you done?" she asks, incensed.

"Nothing, Mother," he fumes. "I didn't do anything."

He runs out the door, enraged. His eyes turn crimson red and suddenly he's transformed into a large black wolf, as Maximus and Trinidad watch in disbelief.

Trinidad turns to Maximus who has tears in his eyes and says, "Our son is no longer our son. He's become a Skinwalker. We must let everyone know before he causes more harm. He's now a threat to our planet."

"I should have known. This does hurt me, Trinidad. I can't believe this is happening," Maximus says angrily.

Back on Earth, Valdivinar and Zapponata are furious as they huddle together in Valdivinar's dark mansion. From his balcony, they see several huge, black-domed buildings filled with many who support them. The sun is glowing in the sky and the temperature is fifty degrees Celsius. He's dressed in an orange thobe and her abaya is black. They are in tears after hearing that Drumpenfeurer was taken prisoner by Maximus. They are also concerned about not having access to oil and minerals.

"What are we going to do, Mother?" Valdivinar asks while smoking his cigarette.

"We're going to go get my grandson from those terrorists," she indignantly answers. "They aren't going to get away with this. Kill Maximus and his son. Whatever it takes. Just do it. Call Chief Manuelito, right now. Have him kill them at once."

"Chief Manuelito, where's my son?" Valdivinar asks him on his wrist phone.

"They never brought him back. I heard they left him with the underground Watchmen," he says as he stands outside the black cave dressed in his Native American clothing. On his head is a red bandana. His face is painted red with black lines.

"What do you mean they left him with the Watchmen? Who are they?" Valdivinar asks.

"They are known as underground humanoids. They are the rulers of the underworld. Their superpowers are far superior to ours. They are technologically more advanced than humans. If you go near them, they will take you to their world for eternity. They do not like humans because they are very jealous of us," Chief Manuelito explains.

One hour later, Valdivinar is inside his large, majestic castle overlooking the five-hundred-billion-dollar luxury mountain resort called Trojenal. It is a big, gray and black structure. Steel apartments are hanging from a giant outcropping in the sand. All the apartments are built next to office buildings. Shopping malls, parks, stadiums, and airports are structured in a straight line.

This unbelievable development benefits many rich people in the Middle East. It redefines business structures, livability and conservation. The lion's share of the money goes to the ultra-rich. This development is best known for stirring up a healthy dose of controversy with its three-hundred-foot-high and twenty-five-mile-long metropolis.

Even though Valdivinar is a controversial figure, he still has a tremendous amount of international support. This ambitious and incredible city he developed for his country is the world's envy. He places fear in everyone who opposes him. Many are killed or placed in prisons if they speak against his regime. His once nice and charming personality quickly changed after three and a half years of his reign. He brought peace and prosperity to the world when he first came to power in Russia. Many willingly give their lives to serve as assassins. It is a cult that has them duped into believing that he is God. All men and women ages eighteen to sixty have to enlist in his army.

Valdivinar believes the end of days inevitably is drawing closer. He fears the end of the world as foretold by the Great Creator. Every day, he strenuously wonders how much longer he has as the world's autocrat.

Hastily, he grabs a radio from his bedroom bureau. Looking out from his balcony, he notices the silver monorail darting past the city filled with people.

"Chief Manuelito, are you there, over?" he shouts.

"Yes, I'm here, over," he answers.

"I want Maximus killed for what he's done to my son. Do you understand me?" Valdivinar demands.

"Yes, of course, Valdivinar. I'll take care of it right away," Chief Manuelito says confidently.

He is a very ambitious Skinwalker who leads five other Skinwalkers. His ulterior motive is to rule Samra. He is a bloodthirsty individual with a heart of ice. Itza-Chu is second in command. He's standing beside him listening to every word Valdivinar says as all six Skinwalkers huddle up ten minutes later, inside the dark cave, planning their attack on Maximus.

"I know how to get to him," Itza-Chu begins.

"Okay, you're in charge of luring him away from El Castillo. We don't have the power to attack him there, with all his protection. We must wait until he is drawn to our cave," Chief Manuelito says.

All Skinwalkers agree and begin to howl.

It is a day of mourning. Maximus is inside the La Azteca Command Center dressed in his blue NASA uniform. Trinidad is with him in a black dress.

He says, "My love, I'm deeply sorry to have placed our daughter in harm's way. She wanted to be an officer so badly; I couldn't deny her that dream."

Trinidad says, "There is much sorrow in my heart. I am very proud of her. She fought bravely for many years. Her sacred name will live forever in our hearts. She is fine. Her new life in Wakan Tanka is free of pain and suffering. This is something we must celebrate, my love."

"You are so right. I'm still flesh and blood with human feelings. She was my daughter. I know I didn't share as many special moments with her as I wanted. She deserved more. But I hope she understands that I was proud of her. Not one day went by that I didn't think about how much I loved her. My admiration for her is beyond words."

"Maximus, life is short for everyone. Stay focused on what you must do for our people. They need a strong leader. You and Chamán are all that's left to make this world better. Itza-Chu lives a life of witchery. Watch yourself. He is unpredictable at this time. Evil is still a dominant and uncontrollable force in the universe. Stay strong, my love," Trinidad says. She fades away.

Ten days later, Maximus is with Magnus walking through the heavily wooded blue, green, yellow, and pink forest ten miles from El Castillo. The huge blue moon called Polaris 10 is glowing ever so brightly. Animal life is in great abundance. The blue and red birds, brown lions and yellow-white giraffes watch them as they pass. The sound of these animals fills the forest. A gentle breeze talks to them as they approach a babbling, rainbow-colored brook, which runs for miles. It is nicknamed "cotton candy" because it looks good enough to eat. Everything is so serene for the moment. It takes away the sorrowfulness of Dahteste's death. Milo sneaks up on them and decides to jump on Magnus' shoulder. Everyone laughs.

They reach the brook. Both men get on a knee and lean close to the brook beside a large, gray tamarack. With their hands cupped, they get some water. They gather as much as they can carry. Drinking the sweet, delicious liquid quenched their parched throats.

"Boy, that's good water, right?" exclaims Maximus.

"Let's fill our canteens," Magnus replies.

Once their canteens are full, they get up and resume walking toward Golthli's hacienda. Red, purple and white Bugambilias decorate his home. Two brown and white palominos are tied on a wooden post by the entrance.

"Good morning," Golthli smiles as he opens the brown wooden door.

He is dressed in a white Gi, his long, white hair adorned with an eagle feather tied to a black leather crown. His gray beard hangs down to the center of his chest.

"I feel great," he says pounding his chest.

At that moment, a "dust devil" appears a few miles away. It looks like a fifty-foot-high tornado moving quickly through the nearby dunes. It sounds like an extraordinary screeching hawk.

"Okay, that doesn't sound too good," Golthli says. "Let's go into the sweat lodge as planned. The hot boulders are ready for the ceremony."

He opens the buffalo skin door to the sweat lodge. Maximus and Magnus enter the dark inipi.

Golthli is heating the rocks in an oven made from adobe twenty feet from the dark sweat lodge. He spoons a boulder out of the oven, placing it in the three-foot hole inside the inipi. He places two more hot boulders in the hole. The hut is filled with hot steam. All are in shorts as they sit around the steaming boulders. Golthli begins humming a Native song in Athabascan.

Fifteen minutes later, Magnus is in a trance, cleansing his mind and spirit. This ritual helps him cope with trauma after each battle. His visions move him greatly today. He takes a little puff of the pipe Golthli hands to him. He sees his father dead on the ground with his brother. Chamán is holding his dad in his arms as he takes his last breath. This is an ominous vision.

He wakes up from the deep trance. His eyes now focus on his father sitting next to him. He can't tell anyone because his dreams usually come true.

After the four-hour ceremony, they are standing outside the sweat lodge. Magnus remains silent. He has always had visions of the unseen world and can see both good and evil ancestral spiritual forces. He can summon his spiritual ancestors at any time, if he chooses. They are the intermediaries between the natural and spiritual realms.

Chamán is indeed a sorcerer and dreaming is a very important skill. The world he lives in is only one in a cluster of consecutive worlds arranged like the layers of an onion. He realizes that even though he has been energetically conditioned to perceive solely this world, he still has the capability of entering other realms. They are as real, unique, absolute, and engulfing as his world. This is accomplished through dreaming, the 'gateway' to infinity. It is Chamán's practical way of putting ordinary dreams to use.

Walking away from Golthli's hacienda, the two wave goodbye. As they pass by the babbling brook, they see a cave in the distance that they hadn't seen before. Curiously, they approach the mouth of the cave, then look at each other. They hear the howl of a wolf. As they walk inside the dark, icy cave, they see no animals. Then they see some figures lurking behind some rocks and wood burning brightly. Large, furry animals with huge, glimmering eyes are walking on all fours. The stench of dead animal carcasses fills the cave.

"Hello, friends," a voice is heard from a Native American man.

He's wearing a brown Apache outfit and a red bandana. His long jet-black hair brings relief to Maximus and Magnus. He is one of them.

"Remember me?" he asks.

Maximus replies, "Chief Manuelito, why are you in this cave?"

He laughs and says, "I've become a bit senile. I prefer living in isolation. Is there something wrong with that?"

"No, I guess not," Maximus says looking at him suspiciously.

Milo starts jumping up and down on Magnus' shoulder. Chief Manuelito is now a few feet away.

"Calm down, Milo," Magnus instructs.

Milo wants to warn him that Chief Manuelito is a Skinwalker but there is no time. Suddenly, two huge wolves creep up from behind Maximus, snarling with their salivating fangs drawn. Maximus and Magnus look in astonishment at the ferocious creatures. Before they step back out of the dark cave, Maximus stumbles to the ground.

"Get him," Chief Manuelito shouts.

Two wolves dash at Maximus and begin mauling his legs.

Magnus quickly says, "Misty, come to me."

His Kevlar superpower suit and helmet instantly drape his body. He's ready for action. However, when he turns to look for his dad, two black wolves are viciously mauling him. Maximus' body is whipped from side to side in the wolves' large fangs. Chamán flies to save him from death.

The wolves turn their sites on Chamán. There are loud thumps as he begins beating both wolves with his powerful fists. He is completely in the fight till the end.

His dad's limp body is motionless on the ground. Milo is tending to him. Chief Manuelito transforms into a brown wolf and joins the attack. One by one, Chamán beats them with his swiftness and powerful fists. Even though the Skinwalkers expertly fight with their large claws, they are no match for the cunning and skilled superhero. He climbs on their backs and rides each one. As the Skinwalkers jerk their heads back and forth, he bounces like a cowboy on a bull ride. He chokes them, having learned the guillotine choke defense from Cochise. He applies the back headlock to each one. Once they are unconscious, they transform into their natural human form.

The coup de gras is to use his silver saber he keeps holstered around his waist. As he jumps on top of each unconscious human, he raises his three-foot saber and plunges it into their heart. With a shriek, they perish.

Then he turns to the last one who is starting to come to. It is Itza-Chu. A flashback of them playing with his sister in his room brings sadness. They were laughing and wrestling like little kids. He pauses to look at him. Itza-Chu is now almost fully cognizant.

He asks, stuttering, "Where are we, great Chamán?"

A second later, Trinidad appears to both of them. She's dressed in a long, black, flowery dress with a black scarf covering her head.

"Mother, what has happened to me?" Itza-Chu asks.

"You are not my child anymore. You've chosen the Ghost Devil over me. You chose to listen to the evil wolf and it turned out for the worst, as I had warned you," she exclaims.

Trinidad turns away and looks at Maximus who lies bleeding to death.

"Look what you've done to your father," she cries.

Itza-Chu sits up and stares at his dying father. Crimson blood drips down his bruised and lacerated face. His body is disjointed and limp as he gasps for air.

"He treated you like no other father could. He gave you everything you needed. You had the world in your hands. Look how you repay him. Why would you want to kill your flesh and blood?"

"Mother, forgive me. I didn't know what I was doing. I wanted to be great like him. If it hadn't been for Magnus, I would have been like him," Itza-Chu angrily says.

Chamán looks at him and drops his silver sword back in his holster. He grabs his gold helmet from his head and takes it off.

Turning to face his brother, Magnus asks him, "What did I do to you to make you this way?"

Itza-Chu looks at him astonished. He says with great remorse, "You're Chamán? You were always better than me, brother. I could never be like you. Chief Manuelito gave me the chance to become a leader of Samra. I wanted the power to rule Samra."

While coughing and spitting blood, Maximus asks, "Did you help kill my daughter?"

Itza-Chu hesitates, but says, "Father, I am ashamed and I cried after I allowed Drumpenfeurer to attack her Star Ship. I loved my sister. I deserve to die."

Maximus finds the strength to grab his silver sword and uses it to lift him. Moving his mangled body closer to Itza-Chu's is very painful. His crippled legs have very little vitality left.

His eyes bleed with anger and anguish as he shouts, "My son."

With his last breath, he falls on Itza-Chu and his silver saber plunges into his heart.

17

· BROOKLYN

"We Indians think of the Earth and the whole universe as a never-ending circle, and in this circle, man is just an animal. The buffalo and the coyote are our brothers, the birds, our cousins. Even the tiniest ant, even a louse, even the smallest flower you can find—
they are all relatives."
– Jenny Leading Cloud

It has been two months since all the bloodshed transpired outside the cave. Cisco is the new Commander of the Samra Space Station. He's wearing an all-gray uniform as he sits at the head of the center table. Magnus, Cochise, Melissa, Golthli, and Master Juno are present.

"Welcome, friends. We've been anticipating word from our brother, Dr. Matthew Hogan, about the next extraction of two-hundred-thousand evacuees from Earth. Our Mother Ships are ready to get going in the next couple of days," Commander Cisco happily announces.

Carol adds on the intercom, "We received word of chaos on Earth. People are dying of famine, viruses, murder, and pollution. There's no medical help except for people who follow Dictator Valdivinar in the Middle East. They will soon run out of natural resources. Oil is nowhere to be found. They keep drilling but the wells are dry. Titanium and aluminum alloys are scarce, so the manufacturing of new battleships has come to an end. The Watchman kept his word."

Melissa says, "What this means is that they'll be looking for other places with these resources. It's well known to them that we have them in abundance. Even though we've lived in peace with little interference from them, we should expect them to attack soon."

Master Juno adds, "We have a million Novatos ready for air and land attacks. Our Boombows are well placed on the perimeter of the city. If they show up, we'll be ready."

Magnus chimes in, "Our ancestors have told us stories about the end of days. I believe the end is coming soon for Mother Earth unless we help her. Her pain is heard throughout the universe. We must overcome any invasion by Valdivinar and his assassins. Maybe someday we can restore our sacred Earth back to health. That can only be done when Zapponata has lost her evil power over the people."

Commander Cisco replies, "I imagine her empire has had enough of us. However, we should never underestimate her. It'll be like fighting a wounded dog. She'll put up a good fight to the end."

Carol says, "I don't see any danger today from other extraterrestrials. All seems calm in the universe, according to our satellite information."

Melissa says, "That's good, Carol. We are still mourning the loss of Maximus. He has passed into the Spirit World. Don't forget about the Powwow this evening. We will be honoring him."

Everyone in the cavernous room rises from the table and solemnly walks out the large glass door.

As the hour of the event approaches, Magnus is kneeling outside the city. He's on a high, flat ridge called Otay Mesa. The sky is dark amethyst and there's a gentle breeze. He's praying, feeling a bit of inner peace listening to the wind and its surroundings. He always believes in looking for sacred signs from animals, people and nature. Like Chamán, he is a clairvoyant and is now recognized as the sole prophet and healer of the people. Then there is peaceful silence as he stares at the colorful landscape below.

Dressed in brown leather Native American-style clothes he says, "Tata, tell me what to do. I am still mourning the death of my father. It's very lonely absent his love."

"Magnus, death is very painful to those who are still in human form," his Tata says. "It is good that you miss him, but remember, he is still alive in your heart. As long as you live and breathe, you show everyone he is still alive. Your father is the GOAT of Samra. He saved millions on Earth from certain death. He will always be a legend in the people's eyes. Never let them forget him. A new monument with a statue in his honor, standing in the coliseum, waiting to be unveiled, will make sure of that."

"Yes, Tata that is what he deserves. He was brave and wise—a great man. He never complained about anything. He always helped others and protected the land."

Tata says, "You are a great man too. It's time for you to go and pay your respects."

As Magnus kneels looking to the universe he says, "There are still millions more to evacuate. We have to bring them home. Home?"

In the midst of despair, his eyes, a deep shade of obsidian flecked with hints of stardust, reflect a profound longing as he whispers softly to the gentle breeze, "Where is home for me?"

Chamán flies to the coliseum for the Powwow celebration. He can hear the loud drumbeats and chanting as he walks inside to watch the event.

The emcee announces, "Welcome, everyone, to the Samra Powwow. We are here to celebrate our new life in this land and to honor the Great Chief Maximus."

The crowd stands, each raising a fist to the sky, chanting, "Maximus. Maximus. Maximus."

At the very center of the marble floor is a twenty-foot bronze statue of his father with a gold headband and turquoise stone on his head. He's wearing his NASA blue uniform with a picture of La Azteca. Both arms are raised and hands clenched above his head.

Chamán says to himself, "Dad, you were the greatest of all time."

The Powwow continues. Dancing, singing and drumbeats are heard throughout the night. Everyone is there to pay homage to a great man.

Thirty days later, a crowded spaceport with two hundred thousand evacuees is disembarking from four NASA Mother Ships.

Carol says in the background, "Welcome to Planet Samra. We have food, water and clothing for everyone. You'll be flown to your new homes in the new city of Del Mar. You'll enjoy the beachfront models recently built for your enjoyment. There is no need for money because everything is free. If you need something, your neighbors will kindly share whatever they have."

Magnus is looking at the miracle of another group of people he just saved. He is now the Commander of La Azteca. Suddenly, he sees a young lady with long black hair dressed in a man's gray hoodie with torn Levis. Her face is covered in dirt. As he looks closer, he sees that she has beautiful green eyes and is around five foot seven inches. She's twenty-five years old. She makes eye contact with him. Confused, she is fumbling around a seat looking for something.

"Miss, what are you looking for?" Magnus asks smiling.

She looks up at this handsome man dressed in a blue spacesuit with a golden eagle embossed on the front. She couldn't take her eyes off it. Then she notices his name engraved on his shirt.

"You're him?" she says in amazement.

"Pardon? Him who?"

"You're him," she says nervously.

"Yes, I am him," he says jokingly.

"You're Magnus, the son of Maximus, right?"

"Guilty as charged, Miss…? What's your name?" he asks.

She stops searching and focuses on him as she stands up to face him.

"My name is Brooklyn, but everyone calls me Brooke," she says politely.

"Brooke, I like that name. What are you looking for?"

She stares at his mesmerizing brown eyes. Then after a few seconds, she says, "I can't find Peanut."

"Who is Peanut?" he asks laughing.

"My toy poodle. I can't live without him," she says desperately.

Brooke turns to look for him, then Magnus brings his

hands forward. After a couple of minutes, she gives up and turns to Magnus. She is surprised as she sees her white, fluffy toy poodle in his hands.

"Peanut," she screams.

Everyone turns around to look at her. Magnus hands Peanut to her.

"Where did you find him?" she cries.

"Actually, he found me," Magnus smiles.

"He found you? Where was he?" she asks, confused and overjoyed to be reunited with her puppy.

For the first time in his life, Magnus feels he is talking to someone special. Perhaps he can help acclimate her to her new surroundings.

"I was walking over to my space car and Peanut started sniffing my leg. I think he's the cutest puppy I've ever seen. Did you come with anyone?"

Fumbling for words, she gently smiles and says, "Well, uh…I came alone. My parents and two brothers were killed in San Diego, California years ago."

"I'm sorry to hear that. My parents and siblings were killed too," Magnus sadly says.

"The great Commander Maximus isn't alive? I wanted so much to thank him for all he's done to save so many of my friends' lives. My people would talk about him as we waited to be rescued. I'm half Navajo from my Arizona tribe."

At that moment, the lights go out inside the Spaceport. Brooke is startled.

Magnus says, "Don't be afraid. I'm here to protect you."

A few minutes later, the lights come back on. Carol's voice is heard on the speaker in multiple languages giving instructions to continue to the awaiting space shuttles outside the Spaceport.

"What did you say?" Brooke asks.

"What do you mean?" Magnus asks, surprised.

"When the lights turned off, you said something," she says in amazement.

"I said, don't be afraid. I'm here to protect you."

"You won't believe it, but my dad said the same thing to me the first night we hid in a dark cave. I was really frightened by Drumpenfeurer's missiles that were blasting the mountains. I was shaking, but we survived."

"Wow, I wonder what that means. What do you say to some good pizza?" Magnus asks to change the subject.

"Let's go. I'm starving. Did you hear that, Peanut? We're going to have some pizza," she shouts.

They board his private spaceplane outside the Spaceport. It is crowded with people loading onto space shuttles. His spaceplane impresses her. Inside, there is room for eight people. It has a screen to monitor the city and the hemisphere. It is still daylight. The orange skyline looks amazing from his vessel.

"Why do you have to watch the stars from your screen, Magnus?" she asks.

"Brooke, we are not alone in the universe. There are many inhabited planets. Our Great Creator created the universe for a grand purpose. There are more stars than there are people. When we were on Earth, we wondered if there was life on other planets. Do you know that there is over two-hundred-billion stars in our solar system? Our sun is known by its Latin name, 'Sol.' Our solar system includes everything that is drawn into the sun's orbit."

She is impressed with his strong voice, his charm, and his wisdom. She asks, "Have you been to other planets?"

"Yes, I have. I've seen life on planets that my father

named: Planet Zohar, Planet Poway and Planet Chapultepec," he proclaims, showing her each planet on the screen. "Would you like to visit other planets with me, Brooke?"

"Of course. It's been my dream to see other places in the universe. I know we aren't alone," she excitedly replies.

Magnus enjoys listening to her strong voice and is attracted to her confidence. Moreover, Brooke's willingness to learn more about the universe makes him wonder if she would be interested in working with him. He remembers how his mom would say the same things.

"I am on my way to the Samra Racetrack," Magnus says. "We can get the tastiest pizza and hotdogs while we're there. Is that okay with you?"

"Well, let me check my calendar," Brooke laughs. "I don't know…Can I trust you?" she says, smiling and gently touching her long black hair with her right hand.

"Is that a trick question? If you can't trust me, you can't trust anybody."

Magnus had never been challenged with this same wit. His unfamiliarity with his feelings for her catches him off guard. He welcomes her confidence.

"I need to clean up first."

"Oh, sure. Let me take you to your place in Del Mar first. You'll have everything you need waiting for you," he says proudly.

"You mean I have a place waiting for me? Who paid for it?"

He chuckles and says, "Well, here on Samra we don't pay for anything. We believe in helping each other. Housing is built for everyone."

"Carol, please say 'hi' to Brooke," Magnus says as he fumbles with the spaceplane's screen monitor.

As Brooke looks at the bright screen, it lights up to scan her eyes. The light is so bright, she covers her face with her dirty hands.

Carol says, "Hi, Brooke. I see you're from San Diego. What a beautiful city it was. Your father was nicknamed after the great Apache leader Geronimo."

"Yes, but how did you know that?" Brooke asks, taken aback.

"When I scanned your eyes, I could see parts of your past life. You miss him, don't you?"

"Yes, very much."

"Don't worry. You are now safe. This is your new home. We will take good care of you. It looks like you have found a great friend already," Carol laughs.

As Brooke turns to gaze into Magnus' eyes, she feels safe and loved. She's looking out the window and sees the majestic City of El Castillo.

"This place is amazing," she exclaims. "Unfortunately, my generation wasn't brought up in a city like this. We had nothing. I lived inside a cave for years. Commander Maximus provided us with food and water. The Earth is desolate and it's been taken over by locusts and bugs that eat flesh and blood. There were underworld creatures that protected us as well. They have superhuman powers that keep us safe. One of them is named Watcher. He was kind to all of us. However, he is scary to look at."

"Yes, I believe I know who you are talking about, Brooke. I met him once. He is our ally and has been helping us. I hope that someday we can live in peace with him," Magnus solemnly tells her.

"How did you meet him? I didn't think they had contact with humans above ground," she remembers.

Magnus is caught between revealing his secret identity and breaking his promise. He has taken an oath to keep his identity as Chamán a secret. His spiritual ancestors are the only ones who can unmask his secret identity.

He wisely says, "Well, you're right. The Watcher is prohibited from interfering with human life. However, there are special circumstances when he is allowed, just like when he helped feed and provide shelter in the caves for you and others."

As they're up in the air, they view the spectacular night sky full of luminous stars and a glowing blue moon. Even though she is still messy and Peanut is in her lap, she can't stop thinking about how fortunate she is to be with this handsome man.

"Look, that's Jupiter," Magnus says. "Do you know that Jupiter is the fifth planet from the Sun and it's by far the largest planet in the solar system—more than twice as massive as all the other planets combined? The orange, white and reddish swirls are cold, windy clouds of ammonia and water, floating in an atmosphere of hydrogen and helium."

"I didn't know that, Magnus. Can you teach me all about the planets? I want to know everything you know about them."

"Of course, I will. It might take some time to teach everything I know. We'll have to hang out together so I can teach you. Maybe you'd like to join us at the Samra Space Station Center. You can learn more about the universe and our space station technological program. Would you like that?"

She couldn't believe what he just said. This person whom she had only met an hour ago wants to be her mentor. She hugs him and kisses him on the cheek.

"Oh, I'm sorry," she says, embarrassed.

Magnus is happily startled and he is in a daze, completely caught by surprise. Trying to remain composed as a leader of the planet, he respectfully says, "Don't be sorry. I've never been kissed by another woman before except my mother. I liked it. I wanted to kiss you too, the moment I saw you hugging Peanut."

"Really? I didn't know. I am so embarrassed being around you because your father is my hero. Look at me. I'm all dirty and my clothes are torn. This is no way to make a good first impression," she shyly tells him.

"Listen, your appearance made a huge impression in my book," he excitedly replies.

"So, you feel sorry for me? You want to help me because I'm alone?" she asks, confused.

"Well, you needed help finding your puppy, right? Remember, it was Peanut who came to me. He brought us together. Do you believe in fate?"

"Fate? You think fate brought us together?" she asks, astonished.

Magnus senses her frustration. He explains, "I believe animals have a spirit like all living things. Peanut's spirit chose to come to me in the crowded Spaceport. He was lost and frightened. He was looking for you. He found me so that he might find you. That is what I believe happened. Do you believe in spirits?"

"I think I do, but I don't know too much about them," Brooke says in bewilderment.

"I believe in the supernatural spirits because I have dreams of my ancestors talking to me. I see them and I talk to them. They have taught me a lot about life."

She understands what he's saying. Her visions are similar to his. She wants to learn what they mean. His wisdom intrigues her.

They arrive at her new place in Del Mar. He glides down to the front of the beautiful blue house on the beach.

"Okay, I will tell you that there is life after death. I'm Apache and my roots are strong," he proudly says.

"The Navajo and Apache people have been friends for thousands of years."

"Yes, that is true. I see and talk to my Tata often. He inspires me and gives me wisdom. He told me he's part Navajo. Enough of that for now. Would you like to meet the only living family I have?"

"Yes, of course," she replies.

"My grandparents, Matthew and Melissa Hogan, work for the NASA Space Station. I love them a lot. My other grandpa is Golthli, an Apache Shaman. I also have a great droid friend named Cochise who's awesome and strong. You're going to be amazed when you see him. I also have a white German Shephard robot dog named Kiki. Last, but not least, is Milo, my advisor who is a monkey," he proudly says.

"A monkey advises you?" she laughs.

"He's not just any monkey. He is one of the smartest living animal spirits I know. What do you think about your new home?"

She walks to the front door.

"I don't have a door key."

"Oh, I forgot to tell you—the screen needs to scan your eyes."

As she moves her eyes closer to the screen, the front glass door swooshes open. They walk inside. Both look around, admiring the beautiful decor. A white leather sofa sits in front of a fireplace. A television is turned on to a classic movie called *Home Alone*.

Magnus says, "This is my favorite movie."

They pause to watch the humorous scene when the young boy is holding a machine gun, telling a man in a gray suit that he is going to pump his gut full of lead if he doesn't get off his property.

After laughing, they walk into her white kitchen looking at the refrigerator filled with vegetables and water.

"What do you think, Brooke? Do you still feel you can't trust me?" he asks sarcastically.

She is overjoyed. She hugs him again. This time, he hugs back and she begins to cry. She hasn't lived in a house in years. Now, she has a free beachfront home for her and Peanut.

Once she calms down, she asks Magnus, "Is there a shower and bathroom?"

"Let's find out," he answers as he takes her hand and walks down a hallway.

Since the windows are slightly open, they can hear the soothing sound of the ocean waves crashing against the rocks. The white foamy water can be seen. There are chirping red and white birds flying above the waves. It is a sign of peace and tranquility to both of them. She feels a strong sense of calm at this point in her life.

In her bedroom, she finds new clothes in the closet.

Then Magnus says, "Here's the shower."

He is waiting on the white reclining leather couch for Brooke. His Tata and mother appear before him.

Tata says, "You have found someone special in your life. She needs your love and protection."

"Take care of her, Magnus, she will bring you much happiness in life," Trinidad adds.

"Thank you for confirming what I feel about her."

"All we can say is that you're meant to be together," Trinidad smilingly says.

Brooke walks into the room and asks, "Who are you talking to?"

They disappear. He's startled by her question.

He stutters, "Brooke, would you believe me if I told you I was talking to my spiritual Mom and Tata? They always come to me in spiritual form when I have questions. I'm able to see them. Sometimes, I think I'm dreaming. I don't quite understand how that happens. I wonder if I'm dreaming right now."

"I understand what you're saying, Magnus. I hope what's going on right now is real because it feels like a dream ever since I met you," she confesses.

This brought butterflies to his stomach. He knows that he is in love. She looks ravishing, dressed in her new white Chiffon V-neck, long-sleeved dress. Her face is clean from the hot shower. She has put on light red lipstick to brighten her soft sultry lips.

"Oh my God, Brooke. You look gorgeous," he says while staring at her.

"Thank you. I'm ready, Freddy," she says jokingly.

"Your carriage awaits my dear," he says as he gently bows to her and points toward the door.

Moments later, they're at the Samra Racetrack eating pizza and drinking lemonade. In front of them is a parade of twelve horses in the paddock. As each horse walks by, the horses' big brown eyes stare at Brooke. She is so excited to see these magnificent animals ready to do battle on the racetrack. Their muscular frame and bright-sheened skin glow under the lights. She can't decide which horse to pick.

She looks at the horses' names on the program. "I like this one," she says as she points to number five. "His name is Chamán The Great."

Magnus couldn't believe she picked his secret identity. What could that mean, he wondered.

He acknowledges, "Okay, let's get a ticket for the number five."

They rush to one of the ten ticket windows as they hold hands. Many people are at the track enjoying the races. It's always a joyous atmosphere watching horses competing. They are very well taken care of and the fans are always thoroughly entertained.

"I'll take a ticket on number five," Magnus says.

The ticket comes out of the machine and is handed to him. He gives it to Brooke who looks at the big number five in purple with the horse's name on it.

"It's now post time," Trevor Big Feather announces to everyone.

Magnus and Brooke run toward the finish line to watch the race. They weave through the crowd and are finally at the rail. They watch the jumbo screen with the horses entering the starting gate. One by one, each is guided by the jockey into position. The jockeys are dressed in different colored silks and hats to distinguish each of the horses. Trevor Big Feather needs to study their silk colors in the program to call the position of each horse as they race. Chamán The Great's jockey has on maroon and gold silks with a gold hat.

This race is being run over the beautiful, yellow, sandy terrain. The distance is one mile. The weather is a perfect seventy degrees with a mild wind. The lights add to the ambiance as they illuminate the entire racetrack.

The gates open and the horses are off and running.

Trevor Big Feather shouts, "And away they go. Catch Me If You Can goes to the lead with Dr. Evil close behind. He has to take up sharply and falls back to fourth place. Ghost Busters moves up quickly to challenge the leader. He's followed by Majestic Hero and Chamán The Great is close behind."

"Go, Chamán," Brooke screams as she watches the race on the jumbo screen.

The crowd is cheering on their horses as they reach the head of the stretch.

Trevor Big Feather shouts, "Majestic hero is ahead by two lengths. Ghost Busters is in second. They have one furlong to go and here comes Chamán The Great. It's now a two-horse race between Majestic Hero and Chamán The Great. They are now neck and neck. Neither is giving an inch. As they come down the wire, it is too close to call. It could go either way as their noses hit the finish line simultaneously. Ladies and gentlemen, this is a photo finish. Hold all tickets."

"What happened, Magnus?" Brooke asks.

"Well, both horses reached the finish line simultaneously. It's very close. Now, the racetrack's photographer will determine who won the race. However, sometimes it's a dead heat. That means both horses are winners."

After several minutes, Trevor Big Feather comes on the loudspeaker and announces, "The winner is Chamán The Great."

Brooke and Magnus jump for joy and hug. Then it happens. They are seen on the jumbo screen passionately kissing. They kiss for so long tears start running down people's faces. Everyone recognizes Magnus and they all give them a standing ovation. The ghosts of Maximus, Trinidad and Dahteste are seen above the new couple. They look on and smile approvingly.

"You did it, Brooke. You won," Magnus says with exhilaration.

This is a moment he'll never forget. His love for horses doesn't compare to his love for her.

"What did we win, Magnus?" she shouts. She knew exactly what to ask once their long kiss ended.

"Okay, you can now take your ticket and redeem it at any store in the city. You can get extra food, water or clothes," Magnus explains.

She looks at him and passionately says, "I love you, Magnus."

"I love you more, Brooke. By the way, what's your last name?"

"That's right. I never told you. My full name is Brooklyn Dueñas," she replies with a smile.

"I have so much to show you here on Samra. What do you say we go see something else?" he excitedly asks.

She is willing to follow him anywhere in the world.

"Okay," she says with a big smile.

They get to his golden, eagle-shaped space car in the parking lot. As they are up in the air, hundreds of silver car planes fill the amethyst-colored sky. Brooke peeks down at the modern city filled with glass and chrome towers. She sees magnificently built steeples and dome-shaped structures. The streets are busy with people walking around in the well-lit metropolis. She feels inner peace for the first time in ten years. Peanut begins to lick her face with joy. He feels her happiness and wants her to know he is pleased.

"The Dodgers are playing tonight. They're my favorite baseball team. Let's watch them play at Maximus Stadium, okay?" Magnus asks with excitement.

"Yes, I want to watch a baseball game."

His space car's headlights illuminate the sky for miles. They feel happy together as they stare into each other's eyes holding hands.

"Magnus, I've never been so happy in my life. You make me feel like I've never felt before," she exclaims smiling.

"I feel the same way. I've been through a lot, but you have alleviated my sorrow."

He expertly steers the wheel of his space car to the right and pushes it forward to maneuver to the stadium parking lot. He finds a parking space close to the entrance.

As they walk toward the stadium gate, the announcer says, "Batting next is the shortstop, Matt Armas." The crowd goes wild because he's the Dodgers' best player.

"Let's hurry. I want to see Matt hit," Magnus says as he takes her hand and lifts her into the air with him.

Her disbelief and fright made her reach for his neck to cling on tightly.

As she hugs him, she asks, "What are you doing?"

The night air hit both on the face as he glides with her through the air.

"Don't be afraid. I got you. We're almost there."

As they land in the right-field picnic area, he walks over to an open spot where they can watch Matt hit the ball. A loud thump is heard as the big black bat connects with the baseball. The crowd stands and cheers. The ball shoots like a cannon blast off his bat, traveling four-hundred-fifty-feet into the left field pavilion. The jumbo screen shows Matt rounding second base with his right index finger in the air.

Magnus shouts, "Way to go, Matt."

"Did you see that ball he hit? That's amazing. He's hit fifty home runs this year. The Giants are going down tonight."

Brooke is still wondering how Magnus could fly.

She says, "I didn't know you could fly."

She gestures with her arms in the air like she's flying. Her head moves from side to side, as she mimics him.

"Brooke, I have the power to fly when I want to. I don't know why. It just happens," he explains.

"Oh. Is there anything else you can do that's beyond normal?" she asks curiously.

"Well, I'm your Superman," he laughs. He is trying to avoid telling her his deep secret.

She laughs. "Sure, Superman," she jokingly says.

The Dodgers beat the Giants ten-to-one that night. It was a great game for Matt who had two home runs and five runs batted in.

As they exit, they see the beautiful blue and gray stadium with a big brown, yellow and white Bald Eagle statue. Melissa with Cochise and Golthli walk out of the stadium too. They see Magnus and Brooke together holding hands, walking to the parking lot.

Melissa says, "Magnus, did you like the game?"

He says excitedly, "Grandma, yes, the Dodgers won again. I want you to meet Brooke. Brooke, she's my grandma, Dr. Hogan. Here is Cochise and my grandfather, Golthli. Remember, I told you about them?"

"We just met. I'm showing her our new city. I'm going to take her to see Milo and Kiki," he continues.

"Brooke, aren't you the daughter of Geronimo Dueñas?"

"Yes, I am. How did you know?" Brooke asks, surprised.

"I knew your father very well. I remember you when you were a baby. He was a great singer and played the guitar. I heard he died in a Drumpenfeurer missile attack. I'm sorry for your loss," Melissa sadly adds.

"Thank you, Grandma Hogan."

"Well, we'll see you later," Magnus says as he's still holding her hand.

They walk holding hands and skipping across the parking lot. They board his space car and zoom off toward his house.

18

THE ZERROTS

"Friend do it this way—that is whatever you do in life, do the very best you can with both your heart and mind. And if you do it that way, the Power of the Universe will come to your assistance, if your heart and mind are in unity. When one sits in the Hoop of The People, one must be responsible because All of Creation is related. And the hurt of one is the hurt of all. And the honor of one is the honor of all. And whatever we do affects everything in the Universe. If you do it that way—that is if you truly join your heart and mind as One—whatever you ask for, that's the Way it's Going to be."
– Lakota Instructions for Living passed down from
White Buffalo Calf Woman

Magnus and Brooke arrive at his large hacienda home next to the Samra Space Center. It is all white, surrounded by green and yellow trees. The ground is yellow with pink and red flowers leading to the entrance. Bluebirds are chirping in the trees. He's no longer alone now that he met Brooke. As he scans his eyes, the sound of the door swooshes open.

Brooke asks, amazed, "Is this where you live?"

"Yes, this is where I live, Brooke. It has five rooms and it's big enough for you to move in if you wish. I'd rather you stay here than be alone on the beach."

She looks at him, wondering what to say.

"Let's take it one day at a time for now," she says. "I'm still trying to adjust to this new life and I'm feeling overwhelmed at this time. You have an amazing life and I don't want to interfere."

At that moment, Milo comes screeching toward Magnus as they enter the living room. He is in a rush to see his Master. Milo always misses him while he is gone. He notices Brooke and her puppy.

He jumps on his right shoulder and says, "Master, it's good to see you again. Where have you been?"

"Milo, I'm fine. I want you to meet Brooke. We just met at the Spaceport. She just arrived today from our evacuation mission," Magnus explains.

Milo looks at Brooke, a little jealous.

"Brooke, it's a pleasure meeting you. Any friend of my master's is a friend of mine," he kindly says.

"Hello, Milo," she says in astonishment. She has never heard any animals speak just like a human. What other secrets does he have up his sleeve, she wonders.

Just then, Kiki, his white robot dog, runs to greet Magnus. He notices Peanut cradled in Brooke's arms. Magnus embraces him, nearly crushing his bones.

"Kiki, how are you, boy?" Magnus asks.

Kiki barks and licks his face. Magnus is rolling on the white carpet with him.

"What a beautiful dog," Brooke says laughing.

"Kiki, that's enough," Magnus says smiling.

"Master, can we talk privately? There's a situation with the

Natives developing in the city of the Obees that needs your immediate attention," Milo informs him. He looks at Magnus, gesturing with his eyes to meet him in the next room.

"Brooke, if you don't mind, please stay. Mi casa es tú casa," he politely says with a smile and a wink.

"I need to freshen up," she says. "Where's your bathroom?"

"It's down the hall, the last door on your left. I'll be right back," Magnus says, and when she's out of earshot, asks, "Milo, what's going on?"

"Master, follow me. They're waiting for you," he says urgently.

"Who's waiting for me, Milo?"

"The new Samra Space Station leaders are waiting for you in the Command Center next door."

"Brooke, I'll be right back, okay?" he shouts as he walks out the door with Milo.

Kiki stares at both of them as the door swooshes closed. Brooke hears him and looks out the bathroom door, wondering what's going on.

Milo and Magnus are outside the Samra Space Station Headquarters Room. Magnus gets his eyes scanned and the gray door swooshes open. Engineers and scientists look toward the door as Magnus enters.

"Hello, everyone. What's going on?" he asks.

He notices Commander Cisco is there with Melissa, Matthew, Golthli, Master Juno, and Cochise on the far side of the room studying a map on a wall monitor.

Commander Cisco says, "Magnus, please come and see

this map of the city of Obe. We need your help."

He makes his way down toward them with Milo on his shoulder.

He continues, "We have a situation in our Native brothers' neighborhood—a snowstorm that's already dropped fifteen inches on the ground. There are also reports of thunderous lightning. The blasts of lightning sound more like nuclear explosions. The wind chill is ten degrees Celsius. General Sentarius is the leader of the Obees, as you know. He would like to talk to us right now."

Magnus says, "Please, let's get him on the speaker."

"General Sentarius, are you there? This is Commander Cisco."

A tall, dark-skinned man with red hair and blue eyes appears on the monitor. He's wearing a white Native dhoti and appears nervous.

"Commander Cisco, the life of the planet hangs in the balance. Our death toll is catastrophic. We must bow to Zagar's wishes or all of us will die. I'm losing thousands of my Obees every day. Zagar's subterranean Zerrots have surfaced again and they are killing us. My Obees are fighting relentlessly. We desperately need your help," General Sentarius shouts.

The satellites beam down live videos of the rainbow-colored, snowy terrain. The Obees are shooting laser blasts with large bazooka guns at twenty-five-foot-high gray spider pods called Zerrots, which have ten steel legs that support a one-eyed head. They are under the command of the evil Zagar who makes and controls them from underground.

"General, we're on our way. Please send us your coordinates as soon as you can," Cisco commands.

Carol announces, "Commander Cisco, thousands of five-foot enemy ant droids are on the ground with laser blasters. There are many hand-to-hand battles on the ground. They also present a major problem. The mission is to defeat the Zerrots and ant droids in the snow, and to bring down the evil Zagar. This is another mission for Chamán. He must target Zagar as soon as he arrives. He will be hard to find since we don't know what he looks like; nor do we know his underground location."

Magnus replies, "I'll make sure Chamán joins us. Commander Cisco, my men are ready to go. They're waiting on board La Azteca."

Just then, Trinidad appears to Magnus in the Space Station Room. "Son, be careful. This area is highly unpredictable. The weather is on Zagar's side. The laser blasters won't work as effectively as the Boombows. Make sure the arrow bombs are used."

"Yes, Mother. I agree. Milo, let's go," Magnus commands.

Magnus and Milo re-enter his house. He sees the beautiful Brooke sleeping on the sofa with Peanut lying next to her. Kiki looks up and Magnus puts his index finger to his lips.

In spite of his best efforts, Brooke wakes up and asks with a yawn, "Where are you going, Magnus?"

With a look of surprise, he says, "I've been called to duty. I should be back in a few days. Please make yourself at home. You need to rest after your long journey."

Brooke is tired. She looks at him and says, "Okay, I'll wait here for you to come back."

Thirty minutes later, Magnus is boarding La Azteca with Milo, Cochise and Golthli. They pass by all their 7000 Eagle Jet Bombers lined up on the dock on the way to help their ally General Sentarius. La Azteca arrives in the city of Obe twenty minutes later. Chamán immediately boards his 7000 Eagle Jet Bomber.

In no time, he's blasting away at the hundreds of underground Zerrots. They are hard to put down with just a few Boombow bombs. Fatal red laser beam blasts shoot out of their single eye. It takes ten Boombow bombs to bring one down. Some end up crashing into the rainbow-colored snow. The loud, long battle in the snow takes its toll. Half of Commander Cisco's men have already been lost in just ten hours of fighting. The laser blasters and tomahawks possessed by his Novatos are not nearly enough to fight the red ant droids and Zerrots. They keep coming out of the ground, replacing the fallen. Fighting continues with no end in sight.

Commander Cisco shows up to fight. With his purple laser blaster and skillful maneuvers, he brings a renewed spirit to his Novatos. Both sides are well-equipped and strategically placed to keep the fight going for a long time. Cisco is seen in his thick purple jacket slashing off the heads of ant droids. Unfortunately, they are also armed with their eye laser that shoots and kills a number of the Novatos. The only way to defeat them is from behind. The ant droids can only see what's in front of them. Any movement in front of them triggers a deadly red laser blast.

Chamán exits his 7000 Eagle Jet Bomber through the open cockpit. As he flies, his gold-laser blaster cuts the legs off several gray Zerrots. Unfortunately, they're replaced with others blasting up to the surface. He glances at Commander Cisco fighting in the snow against ten dark red ant droids and a Zerrot. They shoot at him with their laser blasts, but he blocks them all with his laser saber.

Gradually, he is growing weaker and now must block

eleven red laser blasts simultaneously. His face is covered in sweat as he grimaces in anger and pain. He's down to one knee and is seconds from death.

Chamán points his right fist toward the tired Cisco. He shields the eleven red blasts with his chest. Then Cisco gets up to subdue the ten ant droids by swinging his long black sword powered with a purple laser light. Within seconds, large ant heads tumble to the ground.

"Where have you been, Chamán?" Cisco jokingly asks.

Chamán continues to attack the Zerrot by severing its ten legs off with his laser eyes. It crashes helplessly into the rainbow-colored snow.

"I need to find General Sentarius right now," Chamán tells Commander Cisco.

"Go to the tallest steeple-shaped building in the city. He's on the top floor."

"You need to hold them off until I get back, okay?" Chamán pleads.

"I don't know how much longer we can hold them back, but we'll do our best."

"I need some time to put a stop to this and the General is the only one who can help me find the evil Zagar."

With that, Chamán raises his fist and he is off. The blasts from the Zerrots below create clouds of powder from the snow reducing visibility to zero. However, he uses his X-ray vision to scan the large, gray city—five square miles of steepled and domed buildings. 7000 Eagle Jet Bombers shoot blue laser blasts at the Zerrots and ant droids. There is still sunlight left to help identify the largest steeple-shaped building. Once he spots it, Chamán flies directly toward it and lands on the balcony of General Sentarius' home. He sees a large golden-brown fury droid with big white eyes next to the

General. He is wearing a green army shirt and pants. He has long black boots. He's bald and is half human and half droid.

"General, I'm Chamán. I'm here because I need your help. We don't have much time," he quickly says.

"Oh, yes, I've heard about you and your superpowers," General Sentarius answers.

"I need to know where Zagar is and what he looks like. My people don't know anything about him. Can you help me?" Chamán urgently asks.

"I can only tell you that he's under our city. He creates these monsters down there. He told me to take my people from this area or we'll die," General Sentarius says with great fear in his heart.

"Please tell me how he threatened you."

"Follow me," he says, walking to his office.

Vertical bars of light shine brightly around a white computer on a glass desk. General Sentarius issues a command: "Computer, show me Zagar's last message."

"Sending message now."

In black letters, his message appears in Zankaya, a language unfamiliar to Chamán.

"I need this message sent to our supercomputer, Carol, at our Command Center in Samra. Please send this message right away."

Then, into his wrist phone, Chamán says, "Carol, are you there?"

"Yes, I am," Carol replies.

"I'm with General Sentarius. He's sending you a message. Can you track the computer coordinates for where this message originated?"

Carol says, "I'm checking right now." After only a few seconds, which felt like an eternity, she says, "This message was sent from a computer seven thousand kilometers directly below the surface from where you're standing."

"Thank you, Carol. Thank you, General," Chamán says as he quickly runs toward the balcony.

He flies downward and, with his eyes again acting as flashlights, he begins to bore into the solid inner crust with both fists, triggering earthquakes as he goes, which impact buildings and the Zerrots' sense of balance, most of which fall to the ground. The magnitude of the quakes is enough to bring all fighting to a halt. Zerrots and ant droids fall into large crevices.

Chamán reaches a subterranean metropolis. It's an enormous underground city. The buildings are made of solid gray steel. His x-ray vision spots a Zerrot and ant droid manufacturing plant. There's a creature that looks like a giant, orange, furry, two-armed and two-legged beast. He's around twenty feet tall with an oversized head. There are five-foot ant droids bringing in parts for the production of more creatures.

In his strong commanding voice, Chamán shouts, "Zagar."

The startled huge beast turns around. When he sees Chamán, he warns him, "Do not come any closer or you will meet your doom." His voice is deep and commanding. To Chamán's surprise, he speaks English proficiently.

"My friends on Earth told me that I might meet you one day," Zagar laughs.

"I come in peace," Chamán confidently says. "If you stop terrorizing and destroying our planet, we can live in peace together. There is no need to kill innocent Obees and humans."

"Silence! I am the great and powerful Zagar. No one tells

me what to do. I have been here since the beginning of the universe. I'm all-knowing. I understand you're here to stop me," Zagar declares.

"The Great Creator has brought me here to protect every sacred living spirit including all the planet's natural resources. Just live in peace with us. However, if you want to live by the sword, you shall die by the sword," Chamán warns.

"Peace or sword? What a choice. What is peace? There is no such thing as peace, my brave friend. You're too young and idealistic to understand what peace is. One day, you will truly know what I am saying. Come to me," Zagar commands. "I will make you an offer you can't refuse."

"I'm not here to negotiate with a terrorist," Chamán answers.

"I'll give you command over the planet if you follow me," he claims.

"I will not fall under a spell of any of your temptations. The Great Creator has chosen me as His champion to overcome all evil."

"Oh, so you consider yourself greater than me?"

"It is my sacred duty to bring love and peace to the universe. Many are dying because of you. You must stop and promise to live in peace with us. We will accept you into our tribe. Just stop making Zerrots and ant droids," Chamán says.

"Enough stupidity. I will give you one chance to live in peace on my planet. You must fight me to the death. If you win, you shall have the power to rule over the whole planet. However, if I win, the Obees must leave this region or die," Zagar demands.

He walks around Chamán on his two fury, orange paws, snarling and sniffing. His big black eyes appear menacing. After sizing Chamán up, he knows it is time to stop talking.

There is a long silence in the room. Both stare at each other. Zagar draws his black laser sword. It flashes a red beam. Chamán draws his golden saber with a purple flash. The giant creature swings his red laser light at Chamán's head. He ducks and with a three-hundred-sixty-degree turn, he slices off a piece of his nemesis' facial fur. Then Chamán begins his relentless attack, cutting his foe on the right arm and leg. The monster grunts in pain. The giant beast grabs Chamán by the neck and exits the underground through the open tunnel. There's a huge explosion that the satellites transmit to the Samra Space Station. Above ground, the two are in the thick of a laser battle. The fight is aired to the entire planet.

Brooke is watching the battle on the monitor in Magnus' home. It is the first time she has seen Chamán. She's amazed at his skill and cunning yet frightened by the looks of Zagar. She watches Chamán moving faster than Zagar. With each swing, his purple laser light keeps finding its mark on Zagar's body. Zagar cannot keep up with the powerful movements.

Commander Cisco is close by watching the onslaught of piercing laser flashes cutting deep gashes into the monster's body. Blood trickles down Zagar's huge forehead. His eyes are growing faint. Then, with a last right-hand swing, Chamán cuts his head off.

Brooke looks on in amazement as the Novatos applaud his victory. The Zerrots and ant droids fall dead on the rainbow-colored snow.

The Novatos are shouting, "Chamán! Chamán! Chamán!"

Brooke notices Chamán's flying in circles with his fist in the air acknowledging everyone's applause. His movements remind her of when she flew with Magnus to the baseball stadium. She smiles.

19

JUDGMENT DAY

"May the Stars Carry Your Sadness Away,
May the Flowers Fill Your Heart with Beauty,
May Hope Forever Wipe Away Your Tears."
– Chief Dan George

One week later, Satan is relaxing on his red throne chair smoking a large cigar. A cloud of smoke makes it difficult to see his red horns. Zapponata is wearing a long-sleeved, orange dress. Her curled gray hair hangs down her face. She looks nervous and afraid. She doesn't look at him as she limps into the large Castilian-style room. It's dark and cold.

Satan shouts in anger, "I called for you because I just found out that my great friend Zagar is dead. A young warrior in a gold spacesuit cut his head off and held it in his hand to show everyone. They chanted his name—Chamán. I want his head brought to me. If you can't do it, I will cut yours off and put it on my mantel."

"Yes, Master. I will send my son and his legion of assassins to Samra immediately," she says fearfully.

"You will go, as well. Your son has proven to be unworthy again. He's lost the loyalty of his people. His poor decisions have caused a loss of military spacecraft and weapon production. We need their weapons, fuel, metals, and ships," Satan shouts in anger.

"Yes, my Master. I will make sure your wishes are fulfilled. Is there anything else?" she asks reluctantly.

"Yes, there is. I want full control over Samra's colony, which our Apache enemy created. You will stay to govern under my direction. So, this is farewell. I shall never see you again. Go and get it done this time. Chamán is the son of Maximus."

Satan continues smoking his cigar as he watches Zapponata walk out of the dark room with her back hunched over. The echo of her cane loudly resonates on the black marble floor.

Zapponata is now traveling with Valdivinar on the Mother Ship La Mata Raza II. They're looking out into space headed to Samra.

"My son, we must kill Maximus' son, a.k.a. Chamán, or we will never be able to return home. He is the legendary warrior of Samra. You have been trained and have superpowers capable of killing him. You must be prepared to use them when the time comes," she says.

They look at the enormous monitor on the ship's wall and see hundreds of their gray single-pilot jet bombers parked on their long dock.

"Mother, we've hit a roadblock. Their satellites will detect us as we enter their hemisphere. We'll be sitting ducks. This is what happened last time," Valdivinar warns, sweating and shaking his head.

"Stand back and witness the full destructive force of your father's hand," Zapponata commands.

She picks up a red briefcase next to her and sets it gently on the glass table. Inside is a big red mushroom button connected to an electronic machine. She presses it, triggering the opening of a large gray wall. A loud buzzing sound from the electrical charges can be heard. Inside the room is a nuclear golden light chamber with lightning bolts everywhere. Everyone stares at the electrical charges coming from the silver silos.

"This is our new nuclear power plant reactor. This will not only destroy their satellites but will also speed up our flight. They won't know what's going on. Fire," she commands.

Immediately, the nuclear bombs are launched. Zapponata and Valdivinar follow the bombs' trajectory on a sonar screen and can see Samra's satellites exploding into puffs of white smoke. It takes only ten minutes to bomb all Samra's Space Station satellites. They rejoice.

"Yes, we've taken their ears and eyes to the galaxy. We can move in and destroy them," Zapponata excitedly shouts.

Back on Samra, all solar transmissions and live streaming is lost. Navigation systems that rely on satellites to provide accurate location information are no longer available. Nobody can communicate by cell phone or on the Deep Space Network. All computers are down. Carol is inaccessible.

Magnus is at home with Brooke and their dogs enjoying the videotaped movie *Scarface*. They're resting on the white couch. Milo is on his shoulder asleep. Magnus suddenly sees in his mind's eye a vision of an attack by an evil force in the air. There are spacecraft from both sides exploding. The sky's red glare and bombs bursting in the night air brought him great sorrow.

"What's wrong?" Brooke asks as she watches his legs jerking fiercely.

"I just saw something horrible happening," Magnus says in shock.

Melissa comes into the living room after leaving the Samra Space Center. In a panic, she says, "Magnus, you must go to Golthli's sweat lodge to get instructions from your spiritual elder. Come quickly. Something is wrong with the universe. Our satellites have all been destroyed. We must seek a higher spiritual force for guidance. We need to know who is attacking us. Please bring Brooke with you."

Melissa, Brooke and Magnus enter Golthli's sweat lodge. They sit around the hot boulders, their bodies consumed in heat. Golthli enters the inipi and begins to chant in Athabascan. Magnus transforms his mind into Chamán's. He can see the La Mata Raza II Mother Ship headed toward Samra, with Zapponata and Valdivinar in command. They are bombing their satellites.

"What do you see, Chamán?" Melissa asks as she impatiently sits around the hot rocks.

Brooke can't believe she is calling Magnus Chamán. She sits with her legs crossed, staring at Magnus in disbelief. After four hours inside the sweat lodge, Golthli ends with a ceremonial prayer of strength and protection.

Chamán says, "I see the evil ones from Earth invading us

soon. They have their entire army of assassins."

"How do we communicate with everyone to prepare for battle without a satellite system?" Melissa asks.

Chamán looks deeper at the purple and white sparkles coming from the hot stones.

"Chamán, it is time," Tata says. "This is the final judgment day our Creator has foretold for centuries. You're the Chosen One. There will be bloodshed on both sides. You must bring down Zapponata and Valdivinar. This is the only way to victory."

The effect of smoking the pipe with Brooke just before entering the buffalo-skinned hut helped channel Chamán's thoughts more acutely to his vision. Brooke can see and hear Tata too. Her acute concentration looking at the glittering purple boulders has put her into a deep trance. Tata's voice penetrates her senses. This is a sign for her. She feels a sense of belonging to this family. She is from the lineage of the Navajo people. It is in her blood to understand Tata's ancestral spirit's message.

Tata adds, "You must go to Commander Zoey, General Chuatemoc, Commander Cisco, and General Sentarius. Let them know they should prepare their armies for battle at once. Go now. I'll be with you as your guide."

"Tata, how long will it be until they reach our orbit?" Chamán asks.

"They'll be within striking distance in forty-eight hours."

Chamán comes out of the trance. It is hard for him to understand if he is finally awake or living a nightmare. He looks at Brooke as Golthli opens the sweat lodge buffalo hide door.

They are standing outside watching the hot steam from their bodies evaporate in the cool air. Magnus is in his traditional brown shorts and Brooke is wearing a light green, knee-length, casual dress. After spending four hours inside the sweat lodge, it takes an hour or so to decompress. Brooke reaches for his hand. As their hands touch, he turns to her and gives her a long hug.

"I'm sorry that I didn't tell you. I promised not to tell anyone that I am Chamán. It is for your protection," he solemnly says.

"Oh, don't worry about that now. I saw and heard what Tata told you. What are you going to do?"

"Brooke, I have to go prepare everyone for this invasion."

"I'm beginning to understand what's going on. Good luck, Chamán," she lovingly says as he walks away.

"Come to me, Misty," he commands. In seconds, he transforms into Chamán.

Brooke steps back and brings both hands to her mouth in amazement.

"I must go now and prepare everyone for battle. Zapponata's army will be here soon. We don't have any time to waste. Carol is unavailable for now. Our day of reckoning is near. Grandma, you'll need to give me the coordinates of our Satellite Observatory. I will need your Command Post radio frequency number. This will be the only way to communicate," Chamán instructs.

"Set the radio frequency of thirty-five thousand at twenty decibels and we'll be able to communicate with everyone within the range of two hundred miles," Melissa advises.

"Okay, let's go," Chamán shouts with raised fists.

He reaches Commander Cisco's beautiful white modern home. Cisco is standing outside in his front garden. It's around noontime. The bluebirds are chirping and flying above his house. He looks up at the bright orange sky and watches Chamán land in front of him.

"What's going on, Chamán?" he asks.

"Commander Cisco, we're going to be attacked within forty-eight hours by Valdivinar's assassins. We lost our satellites, so we'll communicate by radio on a frequency of thirty-five thousand at twenty decibels. Have your ship La Victoria ready to launch. We'll be ready for them in the air. I must go and let your men know to join us at the Powwow this evening," Chamán advises. "Let's go."

And just like that, he is flying swiftly through the bright sunlight. He looks around, but there are no spacecraft or car planes in the air. He's now close to the city of Zoey.

"General Zoey," he shouts as he glides through her balcony into her second-story office.

She's dressed in a green military United States uniform with a green beret hat and eagle feathers hanging down the left side of her hair.

"Zapponata and her army will be attacking our planet within forty-eight hours. We need to prepare our Star Ships and ground forces. They've destroyed our satellites, so we'll use radios to communicate. Please set yours at a thirty-five thousand frequency at twenty decibels. I still need to synchronize that frequency at our satellite station," he declares. "Your battleships must be in the air as soon as possible. I must see our other allies. Do you have any questions?"

"Yes, I do. Are they bringing their entire assassin force?" she asks.

"Yes, I suspect they have all of them. After this battle, we will never see them again. I promise."

"Well, at last, my prayers have been answered. I always

wanted to be here to see this final battle against the evil Zapponata and her son Valdivinar. Tell me, what's the plan?"

"We'll need all your battleships up in the air by tomorrow afternoon. They must be on standby to attack from the north. I'll need all your Novatos in El Castillo ready to attack from the ground. They'll be manning the Boombow Station on the north side of the city. They've been trained to use the larger bow. It's going to be a huge undertaking on their part to aim accurately but I've seen them in action. I'm confident in them."

"Chamán, I just want to say that our life on this planet hangs in the balance. Be careful. Don't be fooled by their trickery and lies," she mentions as she waves goodbye.

"By the way, don't forget about the Powwow this evening. We expect you and your men to attend. Let's go," he graciously says as his red cape waves in the calm wind.

There's a streak of smoke tailing him as his velocity reaches one hundred miles per hour. He's looking down at the beautiful forest of brilliant green and yellow trees. The yellow and white giraffes and pink flamingos are grazing by the rainbow-colored brook.

He finds General Chuatemoc sitting in a chair smoking a pipe in front of his one-story chrome house. He's a huge muscular man with long black hair and a beard. His purple-colored headband augments his black jumpsuit and large white tennis shoes. He is a true character, known as a fierce space fighter. He's a legendary fighter pilot who has more kills than anyone on the planet. People call him, "El Indio."

"Indio," Chamán calls to him.

He looks up to see the tall Chamán standing before him. General Chuatemoc stands up and extends his arm and gives him a warm embrace. He is surprised to see Chamán in person for the first time.

"How is it going, bro?" General Chuatemoc asks.

"I wish I had better news, but Valdivinar's army is back for more. How are your men doing?"

"They're ready. My Obees are ready too," he confidently says.

"How many battleships do you have ready to go?"

"Give me twenty-four hours and all one hundred of them will be in the air, loaded with my Obees, my friend," he replies.

"We have everyone onboard for this epic battle; the toughest one ever fought in the history of the universe. Your men and Obees will be our strongest space fighters. We expect a heavy space battle. You're the best we have. We need Valdivinar and Zapponata driven to the ground. For us to have a complete victory, they must be captured alive. With your help, you can force them down to meet me face-to-face."

"I will do my best, Chamán. But I don't understand why you want them alive."

"The Great Spirits demand that I meet with them. I must obey," he responds.

"Okay, I'll make sure I send them to you."

"You're a good man, Indio," Chamán responds, then adds, "I almost forgot to mention that all satellites are destroyed. We will be using our radios on a frequency of thirty-five thousand at twenty decibels. We'll be live in around an hour. We also have the Powwow this evening. We need you and your Obees there to prepare for battle. Thank you, brother." And with that, he launches into the air.

El Indio shakes his head in disbelief as he witnesses Chamán soaring in the air.

Chamán is on his way to see General Sentarius. Suddenly,

a vision of Chief Tecumseh's face comes to him. He is from the spirit world. As a Great Shawnee Chief, he was known as an orator and military leader.

Tecumseh counsels him saying, "Chamán, you are a great man. You have been chosen to help stabilize the universe and form a more perfect world—one that our Great Father always wanted. Unfortunately, the power of the Evil Spirit of Darkness influenced our people's lives. We fought against him to overcome his destructive nature. Live your life so that the fear of death can never enter your heart. Trouble no one about their religion; respect others in their view, and demand that they respect yours. Love your life. Perfect your life. Beautify all things in your life. Seek to make your life long and its purpose in the service of all life. Always give a word or a sign of salute when meeting or passing a friend. Show respect to all people and grovel to none. When you arise in the morning, give thanks for the food and the joy of living. If you see no reason for giving thanks, the fault lies only in yourself. Abuse no one and no thing, for abuse turns the wise ones into fools and robs the spirit of its vision. When it comes your time to die, be not like those whose hearts are filled with the fear of death. Don't weep and pray for a little more time to live. Die like a hero going home." Then suddenly Tecumseh is gone.

Chamán continues his flight, pondering his words.

Meanwhile, Zapponata and Valdivinar are standing by the large window looking at their dog fighters flying around. They're excited about the prospects of taking over Samra and killing Maximus and his son once and for all.

"Mother, we're almost there. They have no way of knowing. I've set the coordinates to fly to El Castillo where they have their Command Space Station. This is where Maximus lives and established the first city. We should find his son with him," Valdivinar says with evil in his heart.

"We must target this area. Once we take over this compound, we should be able to control the city and the entire planet. However, you will kill Maximus and Chamán," Zapponata directs as he nods.

Chamán is meeting with General Sentarius in his home.

"General, we're going to war with our worst enemy. It is our nemesis from Earth. They'll be here within forty-eight hours. We need to know if we can count on you and the Obees to help defeat them" he says.

"What are our chances?" the General asks.

"Our chances look good if we all stand together. I can't tell you what will happen to this planet if they take over," Chamán quickly explains.

"Okay, that says it all. What do you want us to do?"

"Synchronize your radio to the frequency of thirty-five thousand at twenty decibels for instructions from the Samra Space Command Center," Chamán explains.

As Chamán begins to walk away, he says, "We're counting on your Obees for major ground combat with their droids. Don't forget about the Powwow this evening. We expect you to be there."

The General nods and hears him say, "Let's Go," and Chamán is off in a flash.

Chamán is at the Satellite Observatory. There is a five-hundred-meter aperture spherical radio telescope. He goes inside to talk to Naiche, a twenty-seven-year-old engineer in charge of the Observatory. He is from Taos, New Mexico and a member of the Apache Tribe. He has long, shiny, black hair.

"Hello, Naiche. How are you?" Chamán asks.

"Chamán, I'm good. How can I help you?"

"As you know, we lost our satellites. We need to find out what's going on in the hemisphere. We're expecting trouble in the next forty-eight hours. Have you seen anything unusual through Big Bertha?"

"No, I haven't. Everything looks normal out there," he says as he tucks his white t-shirt inside his Levis. This is his home, so his half-eaten Frybread is on his office table.

"We need you to synchronize the amplitude of the antenna radio control to twenty decibels and the frequency at thirty-five thousand hertz," Chamán directs as they walk over to his radio station.

Naiche begins the synchronization on a wall-mounted digital control panel, which he opens by having his eyes scanned.

He says, "Okay, it's set."

Chamán reaches for Naiche's silver radio and turns it on.

"Grandma Hogan, come in, over," Chamán says.

"Chamán, I can hear you," she says joyfully.

"Okay, now we can communicate with everyone on their cell phone, radio and computer to this frequency. We should hear from Carol soon. It'll be the key point for communication."

Melissa dials in the frequency on the computer and Carol

says, "It was difficult not being able to talk to anyone. I had no reception in space because the satellites weren't working. I'm glad you thought of using a radio frequency to create a signal. There's no doubt that Zapponata and her evil son are on the way to take over Samra. More importantly, they want to vindicate the loss of Drumpenfeurer by killing Chamán. They must still think Maximus is in charge."

"Carol, this is Chamán. I need our allies to meet me in the Coliseum in ten hours. We will be hosting a nationwide Powwow to prepare and inspire everyone for battle."

Back aboard La Mata Raza II, Valdivinar says, "Mother, I just met with our assassins and droid fighters. I told them the plan to take over El Castillo. It's set and they're ready."

"Do you think for one second that I trust you? I know better than you what needs to be done," Zapponata tells him.

"Mother, have faith in me. I know what this means to you and father. I will kill them," Valdivinar confidently says.

"You had better. If you don't, we'll be dead," she warns him.

The Coliseum is packed with hundreds of Native American female and male dancers dressed in an array of colored clothing. Eagle feathers adorn their regalia. They range in age from five to ninety-five. The drumbeats and songs create an electric atmosphere. The emcee, Big John, is dressed in a brown, white, blue, and red shirt. He has on Levis and brown boots. His long, shiny, black hair is in a ponytail.

He's forty years old. He's been the emcee of these ceremonies since he was thirty.

Big John says, "Welcome, everyone, to our celebration of life and preparation for battle. I see many have made it from all over the planet. Where are all my brothers and sisters from the Apache Tribe?"

The Apache people let out a shout.

"Where are my brothers and sisters from the Navajo Tribe?"

The Navajo people make a louder noise.

"We're just about ready to start, ladies and gentlemen," Big John continues. "This is what we call our grand entrance. We sing our grand entry song. All our singers, are you ready? All the drummers, are you ready? Okay, let's begin."

The drums are pounded and the singers start chanting the entrance song. There's so much noise it's deafening. Dancers from all nations parade into the Coliseum. Some are dancing as they enter to join those who are already inside.

"Bring in the great message," Big John says. "Let's have a round of applause for Dennis War-Horse as he brings in our final group of dancers. Yeah!"

The ceremony is witnessed by non-native people and General Sentarius' Obees. All allies sit stoically in the stands. The evening turns into dawn. However, the dancers, drummers and singers look like they could go on for days. As is customary, dancers are recognized and awarded for their dancing ability.

Big John announces, "Your fifth-place winner is Joe Little Feather. Your fourth-place winner is John One Star. Your third-place winner is Terry Johnson. Your second-place winner is Ariel Bright Star. Your first-place winner and champion is Matthew Little Hawk. Your winner in fifth place for the ladies is Josie Big Sky. Your winner in fourth place is Laura Lassie. The winner in third place is Karla Clayton. Your winner in second place is Morning Star Redbird. The first-place winner and champion for the ladies is Ozzie Blue Bird. Let's give them a round of applause."

Loud handclapping erupts from everyone sitting in the stands. All participants are greeted with a hug and given gifts by Magnus, Melissa, Cochise, and Golthli at the center of the Coliseum.

20

INDEPENDENCE DAY

May the sun bring you new energy by day
May the moon softly restore you by night
May the rain wash away your worries
May the breeze blow new strength
Into your being
May you walk gently through
The world and know its beauty
All the days of your life
An Apache Blessing

The day finally arrives. It is a cold, stormy morning. The temperature in El Castillo is twenty degrees Celsius. The black clouds cover the view of all spaceships from ground level. Samra's vessels are in place, waiting for the arrival of Valdivinar's fleet.

"Everyone ready?" Chamán calls on the radio onboard his Eagle 7000 Jet Bomber.

His officers commanding the Mother Ships say, "Yes, sir. Waiting for your command to attack."

With his X-ray vision and superpower ears, Chamán can

see and hear the enemy approaching. He announces, "They're around two hundred miles away. They can't see or hear us since they destroyed our satellites. On my command, I want all Eagle Fighters to attack them with the Boombows."

Carol adds, "Star Ships, prepare for enemy contact in sixty seconds. Wait for your Commander's orders. General Sentarius, prepare the Boombows. The clouds are in the way but I trust you'll cause enough damage to their fleet of jet bombers. General Chuatemoc, your mission is to find their Mother Ship La Mata Raza II. Once you locate it, let us know. Chamán must meet with Zapponata and Valdivinar in person."

Both men listen to her commands and acknowledge they are ready, "Yes, Carol. We'll take care of it."

General Chuatemoc is sitting in his chair looking out his Mother Ship window and says, "Engineering room, are you there?"

"Yes, sir. We're ready to fire our missiles on your command," Sonny Little Feather says.

"Sonny, I don't want anybody to fall asleep today. Understand me?" General Chuatemoc demands.

"Yes, sir," he answers.

"Everyone, I see them," Chamán announces from his vessel. "They're now within range to begin firing." His x-ray vision spots them ten miles away. "I see a large gray Mother Ship shaped like a dragon, surrounded by hundreds of gray dog fighters. They are traveling directly into our trap."

Valdivinar commands on the radio, "My assassins, we're entering their city in a few minutes. You have the green light to begin blasting away like you've done so many times. They have no communication or sonar capability, so they have no idea we're here. You're to fire at will. Any living being on that planet must be obliterated. This is a job for a butcher, not for a King. Go and kill everyone."

Suddenly, the first blast is heard and felt by La Mata Raza II. A Boombow bomb hits the starboard side of the ship, causing substantial damage. Zapponata falls on her head as she hits the red marble floor. She lies there unconscious and bleeding from her mouth.

"Mother," Valdivinar yells desperately.

He holds her in his arms as the ship is struck again. Everyone scrambles to keep the ship together amid the smoke and cacophony throughout the vessel. Valdivinar, sweat pouring off his face, regains some composure. As he looks out the window, he sees his entire fleet surrounded by three gigantic Mother Ships and thousands of Eagle 7000 Jet Bombers. They're shooting down his small dog fighters.

"What's happening?" Valdivinar yells.

"Dictator Valdivinar, this is General Chuatemoc," he announces on Valdivinar's radio. "You are surrounded. It's time to give up or we will blast you and your assassins to kingdom come."

"I will never give up. You have no power to take me down," Valdivinar says as he walks over to his battle station in front of the large window of the ship.

He begins pressing red buttons on the control panel. Blasts of gigantic red-light beams come from all corners of his spacecraft. Hundreds of Eagle 7000 Jet Bombers are instantly destroyed. General Chuatemoc's huge vessel and entire fleet are gone.

"General, are you there? Over." There is no answer as

Carol continues, "Commander Cisco is going to back you up in five minutes."

Still, there is no response.

Carol tells everyone, "General Chuatemoc is gone."

A huge explosion is heard inside the Samra Space Station. Brooke is inside sitting nervously, holding Peanut. The blasts above are relentless. She views the array of multi-colored lights from the missiles from both sides turning the orange sky into a fiery inferno. Bombs are landing close to Magnus' home. This is what she was used to while hiding in a cave in New Mexico.

The fighting on Samra lasts for hours. She watches bomber jets from both sides fall from the sky as she peeks out the window.

Melissa and Trinidad can't see much without their satellites as they wait inside the Samra Space Station. However, they hold tightly to the furniture when the walls shake violently.

"Assassins, we need to find the Samra Space Station as planned," Valdivinar shouts angrily.

His engineer answers, "Sir, we're directly above the station."

"All men, board your jet bombers and prepare to land. Get my jet bomber ready," Valdivinar commands. "The fight will now take place on the sandy terrain."

In the City of El Castillo, Obees from General Sentarius' army are fighting valiantly against Valdivinar's gray human droids and assassins. Eye blasts of white light coming from the Obees bring many assassins down, though they are incurring great losses as well. The enemy droids' red-eye blasts are just as deadly and kill many golden Obees.

Commander Cisco says, "Men, let's go after La Mata Raza

II. We need to surround it and take control. Most of their assassins are fighting on the ground. It looks like they want to take control of our Space Station. Carol, I see them outside your door. Let everyone know, you're the targeted site."

Chamán is flying toward the Space Station. As he comes near, he can't believe the city has almost been completely destroyed. There's screaming throughout the streets; cries of mothers' pain and suffering for their dead family.

Mothers are holding their dead babies in their arms in front of their half-destroyed homes. Many dead humans and Obees are sprawled on the yellow terrain. The buildings are smoking and the stench of blood fills the air.

He quickly removes his helmet for an eye scan outside the Samra Space Station. The door opens and he's shocked at the sight. Valdivinar and ten of his assassins are holding Brooke and his grandmother hostage. Valdivinar has his black lightsaber drawn and the red light is aimed at Brooke's face.

"The Great Chamán is none other than the son of Maximus. How fitting that the son of my father's great nemesis has been bestowed with great powers to protect these weak and pathetic humans. I just found out your father is dead," he says laughing.

"Valdivinar, I understand your mother is injured onboard your abandoned ship, right?"

Valdivinar glares at Chamán and calls to his ship with his wrist phone. "Anyone there? Come in, over."

To his horror, it is Commander Cisco who answers. "Nobody is here that can help you, Valdivinar. I've taken over your ship and have an old, injured woman you left behind."

"Who is this? What have you done to my mother?" Valdivinar asks nervously. His forehead is drenched in sweat as he walks toward Melissa.

"Very well. Is this what you call a Mexican standoff?" he says in an evil tone.

Chamán says in his strong, deep voice, "Let go of the women. This is between you and me, isn't it?"

Chamán stares deeply into his eyes. Valdivinar is hypnotized for a moment. However, he has the power to resist. He shows off his own skills by disappearing and reappearing behind Chamán.

"Don't be afraid, Magnus. I won't make you suffer. It'll be quick," he says, pointing his saber red light at his throat.

"My name…is Chamán," he exclaims as he puts his helmet back on.

Brooke gasps for air as she says, "Don't you dare hurt him."

"Oh, wow. This is better than I imagined. She loves you. You would serve a great purpose for me, my dear," Valdivinar tells her. He stares at her while licking his lips with his long, forked, black tongue.

"Don't you lay a finger on her. This is between you and me. Let's settle this man-to-man," Chamán demands.

"Man-to-man? Are you sure, my little courageous man?" Valdivinar asks with an evil hiss.

"Commander Cisco, come in, over," he speaks into his wrist phone.

"Yes, Chamán," Cisco answers as he stands over an unconscious Zapponata.

"I need you to bring Zapponata to me right now," he says in a commanding voice. "We're inside the Space Station."

"Yes, Chamán. I'm on my way," he replies.

Cisco picks her up from the floor. He carries her to his jet bomber parked inside the vessel's dock.

As they board together, she regains consciousness and

demands, "Who are you?"

"People call me Cisco," he calmly responds.

"Where are you taking me?" she angrily asks.

"I'm taking you to see the Great Chamán, our leader," he replies with a commanding voice.

"Oh, I wish to see him too. Where is my son?"

"Your son is with Chamán," Cisco says as the vessels head toward the Space Station. They arrive and enter through the compound door.

"My son, how are you?" Zapponata immediately asks as she stands holding on to Cisco for support.

"Mother, I'm okay. I'm glad to see you are feeling better," Valdivinar happily says.

She stares at Chamán in wonder. "So, you are Chamán? You've caused me great trouble with my Master. Did you know?" she says as she looks at Brooke.

Chamán sternly declares, "You are the reason my family is dead along with billions of others. Do you deny that?"

"Of course, I don't deny it," she wickedly says. "It's been my mission in life. It's part of war. People die. One cannot run from what they are supposed to do in life, wouldn't you agree?"

"Well, we all have a purpose. Our Great Creator has chosen me to protect all people from evil. I am prepared to give my life for them," he replies.

"Well said. How do you plan to lead and protect my people? You have no experience as a politician," she remarks.

"They are not your people anymore, Great Demon. They want to live in peace and harmony, not in turmoil. We don't have to pay taxes or worry about health plans. People help each other. If someone needs something, we help them. There are no pharmaceuticals on this planet. Health problems are handled naturally as they were when life first began," Chamán eloquently explains.

"You impress me, child. But we aren't leaving until you are dead. I made that promise to my Master. I always keep my promises. Do you understand?" she ominously tells him as her eyes turn bloodshot red.

Chamán is suddenly surrounded by his spiritual ancestors to his great relief. Tata, who stands six feet four inches tall, smiles at him proudly.

"This is your greatest moment," Tata says. "We have waited for this day since the creation of man. What happens next will forever change the universe. If you listen to your heart, He will come."

"Who will come, Tata?" Chamán asks, confused.

Chamán looks up. With his arms lifted he begins to chant in Athabascan. Zapponata and Valdivinar do not understand what he's saying. They begin to laugh. Chamán's body shakes as the Great Spirit speaks to his mind.

"The hour has come. I've heard my children's cries for help for too long. I will put into your heart what needs to be done, my brother," the Great Spirit tells him.

He turns to face both villains and says boldly, "You have been charged with crimes against humanity. For that reason, you must be put to death, according to the law."

Everyone looks at him in amazement. A white light glows around him as he speaks.

"I challenge your best warrior to a fight-to-the-death match in our coliseum. The winner will get the retribution he craves. Do you accept?"

"We accept your challenge with one condition," she replies.

"What condition?"

"That everyone must return to Earth when you are defeated," she demands.

"Your condition is accepted. Who will be your challenger?" Chamán asks.

"I am your challenger," Valdivinar quickly answers.

"Very well. I will see you in the Coliseum in five hours," Chamán says.

Carol announces on the radio, "People, the greatest fight in the history of the universe will take place in our Coliseum in five hours. It is a fight to save you from the evil power of Zapponata. Please come to support Chamán as he defends your right to be free."

Five hours later, the Coliseum is packed with everyone who can find a seat. Those who can't are standing outside watching from a jumbo screen. Drums beat profusely and Native Apache songs are chanted loudly. The lights go on as it begins to get dark. The bright blue stars illuminate the amethyst sky. It's windy and cool. The temperature is twenty degrees Celsius. Native dancers dance with colorful feathers, their clothing swaying in the wind.

Brooke is standing next to Chamán inside the locker room. He's dressed in his shiny gold superhero suit. His silver saber sword hangs from his belt. Milo is on his shoulder.

She anxiously says, "Chamán, please promise me you'll be okay. I don't know what I'd do without you. Promise me you'll be back. I can't go out there and watch. I'll wait for you right here."

"Brooke, you have given me more courage than I've ever had. I can't say if I'll be back, but I want you to know that I love you with all my heart," he says as he hears Carol's announcement for him to come to the center of the arena. He hugs her and whispers, "Don't be afraid. I'll be back."

Chamán rushes out the door and the crowd gives him a standing ovation as he enters the arena. He's standing with Master Juno, waiting for his opponent's entrance. Valdivinar and his mother walk to the center of the arena. He is wearing a dark orange uniform with an orange helmet and matching boots. She has to limp with a cane.

The crowd reacts with choice words and boos.

Zapponata grabs the microphone from Master Juno and says, "My children, it's so good to see you again. I've missed you. I can't wait to take you back home where you belong. You're very special to me. I pray that we are victorious today so that you can once again live in peace."

Loud boos are heard in the Coliseum.

Master Juno takes the microphone and says, "Ladies and gentlemen, today's battle is to the death. The winner will decide our fate. Are both fighters ready?"

Both nod.

"Begin fighting," Master Juno says as he walks away.

Chamán slowly pulls his silver saber from his belt. It illuminates in a bright purple light. Valdivinar reaches for two sabers. His are bigger with red strobe lights. He's also a much larger man. He looks down at Chamán with a smirk on his face. Valdivinar twirls both weapons in circles rapidly. Their deadly laser beams clash with sparks of white lightning flashing everywhere. The crowd gasps with every bang.

Chamán is struck on the right hip. He kneels momentarily, grimacing in pain. Then he quickly raises his laser to block a blow to his head. Valdivinar twirls and strikes his foe on the back. Chamán is down on the ground gasping for air.

Valdivinar raises his arms in victory to the crowd who watch in trepidation. Suddenly, Chamán whips his purple beam, severing Valdivinar's left leg. He falls to the cold hard marble floor. Chamán stands above him, breathing heavily.

"Do you give up, Valdivinar?"

"Never," he exclaims and disappears.

Valdivinar quickly reappears in the air behind Chamán. He grabs him around the throat and starts choking him with all his might. He swings Chamán in circles like a windmill, then releases his tight grip, sending him crashing to the hard floor. Chamán is hurt badly. He desperately tries to get up as the crowd begins to call his name. He feels energized by the crowd. He looks at Valdivinar and shoots two bright rays of light from his eyes, blinding his nemesis for a few seconds.

By now, they've been dueling for thirty minutes. Chamán leaps high into the air and comes down with full force attacking Valdivinar's head. To his surprise, Valdivinar, who is highly skilled and has great agility, manages to evade the attack. The saber battle continues for another ten minutes on the marble floor, with dodging and weaving by both combatants. Then Valdivinar begins to play with Chamán. He disappears and reappears on the jumbotron screen platform above the crowd. He waves his sabers at Chamán, signaling him to fight on the steel platform. Chamán points his fist at him and jets toward the jumbotron screen. He's able to fool his opponent by tanking him off the platform, his hands on Valdivinar's neck, who is now gasping for air. Chamán soars skyward, maintaining his tenacious grip on Valdivinar's neck. His chokehold makes it hard for him to breathe. Valdivinar ceases all movement and Chamán releases his strong hold.

The crowd can see them a couple of miles up in the air. The amethyst-colored sky brightly lights up the night. As

Chamán drifts down to the center of the arena, everyone watches and cheers. He holds Valdivinar in his hands. He gently places him on the ground. As Valdivinar lays on his back, Zapponata kneels to see if he's still alive.

"Valdivinar, wake up," she says as tears roll down both cheeks. "Oh, please don't die, my son. If you die, I'll die at the hands of your father."

As Chamán begins to walk away, Valdivinar wakes up and says, "Where are you going, son of Maximus? I'm not dead."

"Kill him, my son," Zapponata commands.

With his back turned to them, Chamán is looking at a bright, round light coming down from the amethyst sky. As it gets closer, he sees the physical Spirit of a dark, slender bearded man dressed in a white robe. He has long, gray hair. His hands are in the air signaling him to remain calm and quiet.

He says, "I have seen enough suffering, my brother. You are a faithful servant of the Highest Order. Stand back as I reveal our Great Creator's wrath once again."

Everyone in the Coliseum can now see Him. Looking at Zapponata and Valdivinar, He says, "You have chosen to act as lawless sinners against my Father's people. Your time has come to an end."

"No, please don't take us away from here. Give us another chance," Zapponata screams as she drops to her knees.

Suddenly, the Great Spirit breathes on them. They vanish in a black cloud of smoke. The crowd stands bewildered. Then the drumbeats are heard and the beautifully feathered dancers start dancing again on center stage. The victory ceremony has begun.

Chamán transforms back to Magnus. He walks into the locker room. His face is bruised and swollen. One of his eyes is partially closed from the hard punches. He finds Brooke kneeling by a bench praying. She looks up and is shocked to see him in such pain. He's standing by the metal door. She goes to him crying. They embrace for a few minutes.

Magnus tells her passionately, "I finally can go home."

She looks at him with tears falling from her green eyes and says, "Me too."

They kiss and walk out of the locker room down a long well-lit tunnel, holding hands.

ABOUT THE AUTHOR

B.N. Armas was born in San Diego, California and raised in San Ysidro. He's a tribal member of the Chihene Nde Nation of New Mexico. He holds a Master's Degree in Educational Administration and an Educational Specialist Degree from Point Loma Nazarene University. He began writing his debut novel after years of researching his family's tribe. His fascination for his Native roots were inspired by his mother who was proud of her Indigenous heritage.

When people think about Native American culture, they often assume it is a unified belief system, but this is far from the truth. Tribes and nations across North America are diverse in both geography and thought. Stories told by the elders encompass many aspects of the culture, natural (and supernatural) creation myths, hero tales, cautionary warnings, and family histories, all of which hold great significance.